"Nothing about me is for sale, lady. Not my time, not my effort and certainly not my compassion."

"I...I didn't mean to insult you." Felicia swallowed hard. "But I'm going to Las Vegas. And if you won't help me..."

"I said I wasn't for sale. That doesn't mean I won't help you."

"But why would you?"

Ethan gave her half a smile. "I have my reasons...."

"Well, all right. It's a deal." She thrust out her hand to him.

He glanced down but kept his hands firmly on his hips. "Not so fast. Before I agree to be seen traipsing over the countryside with a fugitive bride, I'm going to insist on one condition."

Felicia wet her lips. "I don't like ultimatums."

Ethan shrugged. "You don't have to like it. But if you even hope to pull this off, you *will* agree to my terms."

Dear Reader;

Silhouette Romance begins the New Year with six heartwarming stories of the enduring power of love. Felicity Burrow thought she would never trust her heart again—until she met Lucas Carver and his darling little boy in *A Father's Vow*, this month's FABULOUS FATHER by favorite author Elizabeth August.

Love comes when least expected in Carolyn Zane's *The Baby Factor*, another irresistible BUNDLES OF JOY. Elaine Lewis was happy to marry Brent Clark—temporarily, of course. It was the one way to keep her unborn baby. What she didn't bet on was falling in love!

Karen Rose Smith's emotional style endures in *Shane's Bride*. Nothing surprised Shane Walker more than when Hope Franklin walked back into his life with a little boy she claimed was his. Loving little Christopher was easy, but trusting Hope again would prove a lot harder. Could Hope manage to regain Shane's trust and, more important, his love?

The sparks fly fast and furiously in Charlotte Moore's *The Maverick Takes a Wife*. When Logan Spurwood fought to clear his name, Marilee Haggerty couldn't resist helping him in his search for the truth. Soon she yearned to help him find strength in her love, as well....

And two couples discover whirlwind romance in Natalie Patrick's *The Marriage Chase* and *His Secret Son* by debut author Betty Jane Sanders.

Happy Reading!

Anne Canadeo

Please address questions and book requests to:
Silhouette Reader Service
U.S.: 3010 Walden Ave., P.O. Box 1325, Buffalo, NY 14269
Canadian: P.O. Box 609, Fort Erie, Ont. L2A 5X3

THE MARRIAGE CHASE

Natalie Patrick

Published by Silhouette Books
America's Publisher of Contemporary Romance

To the ladies who helped me whip this book into shape without beating up my ego: Beth Harbison, Deanna Mascle, Janella Price and Tamara McHatton.

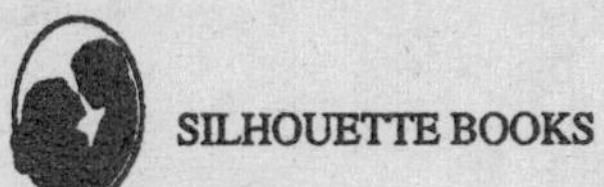

ISBN 0-373-19130-8

THE MARRIAGE CHASE

This edition published by arrangement with Harlequin Books S.A.

Printed in U.S.A.

Books by Natalie Patrick

Silhouette Romance

Wedding Bells and Diaper Pins #1095
The Marriage Chase #1130

NATALIE PATRICK

believes in romance and has firsthand experience to back up that belief. She met her husband in January and married him in April of that same year—they would have eloped sooner but friends persuaded them to have a real wedding. Ten years and two children later she knows she's found her real romantic hero.

Amid the clutter in her work space, she swears that her headstone will probably read: "She left this world a brighter place but not necessarily a cleaner one." She certainly hopes her books brighten her readers' days.

ETHAN AND FELICIA'S MARRIAGE TRAIL

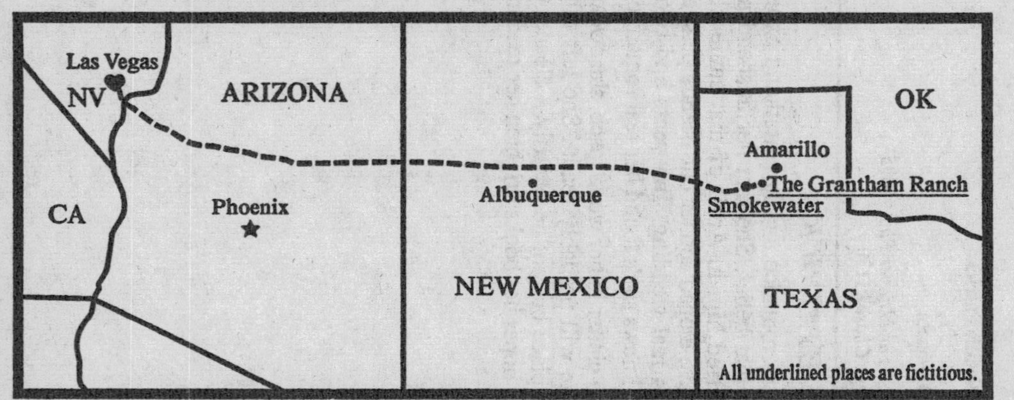

Chapter One

"Damn Gower Grantham and his spoiled brat of a daughter." Ethan Bradshaw glared at the chauffeured car speeding toward him. The sleek limo swerved, following the winding road that separated the Grantham ranch from the only scrap of land he'd managed to keep out of the business mogul's hands. Ethan knew damn well that the presence of that car heralded one thing: trouble.

Miss High Horse, as he'd nicknamed Felicia Grantham when she'd been just an adoring adolescent nipping at his heels, had *arrived.*

Her appearance at her father's sprawling ranch would inevitably be followed by visitors and parties and a lot of society nonsense. That meant an unceasing parade of vehicles rolling up and down the single road just a stone's throw from where he planned to build his new home. Damn.

He turned his back to the red taillights streaking into the distance and adjusted his dusty black Stetson to fit down over his eyes. It didn't do much to keep the howling West Texas wind off his face, Ethan thought glumly. He squinted across the seemingly endless plain, painted eerie blue by the moon-bright night. A few feet in front of him, a campfire popped and crackled. Light and shadow danced in a chaotic circle on the ground around the flame. To his right, his horse pawed the ground. The leather saddle groaned and the metal bridle bit jingled.

"I know, Hickory. You think it's time to call it a night." He sighed and glanced at the battered silver trailer before him. He didn't savor the idea of trying to sleep in the circa 1960 model tin can of a mobile home with that everlasting wind buffeting it all night long. Not that he hadn't slept in worse. In his many years as an international reporter, he'd bedded down in plenty of places that made the clean, compact trailer seem like a sparkling palace.

A particularly filthy hotel in a war-torn Third World country sprang to mind and a slow smile eased over his tight lips. The accommodations might have been just short of life threatening, but his work had been near brilliant—and he had the Pulitzer to prove it.

However, that life was behind him now. Thank God. His new life, the one he'd begun just today, was here on the remnants of his father's ranch in the Texas panhandle. Here, he intended to build the log cabin he would call home. That, and maybe find a down-to-earth girl to marry and help him raise a family.

Ethan stood and stretched his long legs in his work-worn jeans. He chuckled at the irony of his own thoughts. He'd spent his childhood dreaming of escaping these empty spaces and most of his adulthood avoiding marriage. Now, age, and a tidy little nest egg that afforded him this life-style change, had changed his perspective.

A stern gust of wind whipped around the trailer and pressed against Ethan's broad back. He hunched his shoulders. The stiff fabric of his denim jacket grated against his whisker-roughened jaw.

"Guess I can't put it off any longer," he muttered. He kicked at the red-brown dirt with the pointed toe of his cowboy boot. His first night alone on the range had come to an end.

Not that he was strictly alone. He clucked softly to his horse, then narrowed his gaze on a cluster of tombstones fenced in by wrought iron.

The old family graveyard had always been within "spittin' distance," as his grandfather would say, of the family home. His father had torn the original ranch house down years ago but the graveyard stood in silent testament to his family's mark on the Western frontier. In it lay his great-grandparents and several of the children they lost trying to establish the Bradshaw homestead. Now, their graves kept this piece of Bradshaw land in the family's possession.

Ethan scuffed a cloud of dust onto the last ember of the fire. Suddenly, sky and earth melded into a blackened canvas, illuminated only by the pale April moon—and the unnatural glow from Grantham's place almost a mile away.

He grit his teeth, ready to grind out another curse on the Granthams, when something made him stop. He squinted hard across the desolate panorama. A movement caught his eye. Then nothing. Had he imagined it? Moonlight on the plains had caused many a cowboy to imagine all manner of things. Even now, the hazy light cast an ominous spell over the graveyard, washing the aged gray headstones until they appeared bleached white and freshly set.

If he let himself, he could relive the fears of his childhood. Many nights he'd sat staring out his bedroom window at the markers jutting up from the gently rounded graves, waiting for apparitions to appear. Something moved in the distance. A chill rattled his spine.

"Kid's stuff," he muttered. Ghosts and goblins didn't scare him. In his work, he'd witnessed the real demons of this world—death, poverty, indifference and despair. What could be out on the plains to rival that?

He studied the horizon again. Again a flash of movement. Moonlight reflected off something in the distance. Ethan didn't know what the hell was out there. But it was real and in a big hurry.

"Steady," he whispered to Hickory. Ever so slowly he crept up alongside the animal. His career might have taken him around the globe, but he'd grown up right here and had never forgotten the unwritten rules of ranch life. He curled his fingers around the butt of the rifle holstered beneath the horse's saddle. The solid weapon whistled quietly as he unsheathed it from its leather case.

The harsh realities he'd confronted in his line of work had given him a heavy dose of disgust for most guns, but out here a man needed one. A rancher relied on his rifle as a tool. Luckily, Ethan hadn't forgotten how to handle the weapon. He also knew that his considerable skill as an amateur photographer would make the rifle that much safer—or deadlier—as needed. He knew how to keep his eyes trained on the target and to wait for the moment.

He centered the gun sight on the nearly translucent wisp of white floating above the ground between Grantham's ranch and his own property. The shape stilled. He held his breath. Filmy white trails flailed in every direction from a larger white mass, still too far away for him to identify.

For an instant he thought it might just evaporate, or at the very least, decide to veer clear of him and his trailer. He relaxed his finger on the rifle trigger and lifted his head, wanting to get a better look at the thing.

Suddenly, an engine revved at Grantham's place. The wind picked up the angry sound and sent it swirling out over the plain. The form twisted from one side to the other, perhaps agitated by the noise. Ethan held steady and waited. The shape made several frantic gyrations, then stilled for only a second before barreling straight for him.

His heart leapt to his throat and expanded into a hard knot, but he kept his outward cool. Closing one eye, he got the charging figure in his sights again. What the hell could move so swiftly above the ground yet seem to have no definite structure? That's when he heard the hoofbeats.

"You damned idiot," he muttered. "It's something white sitting on a black horse." He kept the white form in the cross hairs. Probably Grantham's idea of a practical joke to "welcome" him home, he thought. "Well, ha ha, Gower old boy. You threw the fear of God into me but good, for a couple seconds."

The ebony horse came headlong into view. Atop the animal, the gossamer-wrapped outline began to take on a definite form. Ethan raised his head. Could it be?

"Oh, good Lord." He holstered the rifle hard and Hickory flinched.

The horse and rider bore down on them. Ethan swung into the saddle only moments before his make-believe phantom reached him. A length of sheer white silk tore loose from the figure's head. It snapped in the wind, then whipped around Ethan's face and throat. He pulled it free just as the horse and rider passed.

Above the thunder of hoofbeats, a screech to rival any banshee's pierced the night. Though he hadn't seen her clearly, he knew this was no specter from the netherworlds. He examined the expensive cloth in his hands. Yep, it was the devil's own daughter, Felicia Grantham, up to one of her antics already—and in a bridal outfit, to boot.

Ethan cursed between his clenched teeth. He glanced at the nearby road just as Grantham's ranch truck raced by. Whoever was driving showed no concern for the escapade taking place on the darkened plain.

"Guess that leaves the rescuing of the galloping bride up to me," Ethan muttered. He glared after her.

How many times had he seen her wreak havoc in these parts over the years? As a child, her temper tantrums were the stuff of parental nightmares. Eight years her senior, he'd had little to do with her then. But not long after her sixteenth birthday, Miss Grantham had decided to test her sex appeal on him.

He'd laughed right in her pretty face—to keep them both from making the kind of mistake that could have ruined their lives. It was no surprise that after that she became distant. With regret, he watched her change. She resorted to snobbery and then the occasional tempestuous stunt to ensure she always got her way. Even now, her pampered life-style and feisty feuds with her superrich father placed her on the cover of the tabloids once or twice a year.

This was probably just another prank, he supposed. Probably. He shifted in the saddle. Hickory whinnied. On the road behind him, a second car tore away from the Grantham ranch.

He had no business getting involved in this, he reminded himself as he clicked loudly and urged his horse to follow the errant rider.

"Whoa, horse! Please whoa." Felicia Grantham clutched the neck of her skittish mount. The horse's coarse mane slapped her in the face and tangled with her own black hair. A gritty blast of wind ripped away another of the many silken scarves cascading from her headpiece. Why, oh, why had she ever thought she could ride this huge animal bareback and with no bridle?

She hadn't thought. That was the answer. She'd merely reacted. Her father had hurt and humiliated her by dragging her away from a wedding chapel in Las Vegas. A quick hop in his private jet and a speedy ride in his car delivered her precisely to the dead center of nowhere—the ranch he'd bought as his private getaway. He'd assumed that of all the places in the world where he owned property, this one could contain her. He'd intended to hold her here until she either came to her senses or her fiancé got bored with waiting and found another wealthy victim to take advantage of.

Once again, her father had vastly underestimated her and her determination to marry Todd Armstrong. Nothing would stop her from carrying out her plans. The horse veered suddenly, sending her bottom bouncing against its unyielding back. The slamming punishment jarred her tightly clenched teeth. Nothing would stop her except an untimely death, she amended.

She thought of the cowboy she had almost plowed down moments ago. She shut her eyes and murmured, "Please, whoever you are, you're the only one who can save me now."

Her heart pounded out an erratic rhythm in her throbbing temples. Wait. That wasn't her racing pulse. It was a second set of hoofbeats closing in. She lowered her cheek alongside the horse's neck to peer behind her. Through the darkness, she could make out the shape of the unknown cowboy in hot pursuit. She whispered a thank-you to the heavens.

"Whoa, boy, whoa," the cowboy commanded. Immediately, her horse's pace slackened, if only a little.

Felicia had no trouble understanding why the near-frantic animal would respond to the stranger's deep, soothing voice. Something in that definitively masculine tone demanded trusting surrender. She relaxed a little herself, enough to allow her body to straighten.

The horse beneath her seemed to sense her restored confidence and again it slowed. Still, she had no means of controlling the beast.

"Get a better grip on him," he shouted above the raging wind. The cowboy demonstrated by snagging up a handful of his own horse's mane.

Felicia wove her fingers in the stiff black hair. It cut into her palms and slashed at her wrists, but she held on.

"Now, pull back, let him know who's boss," he bellowed. "Tell him to whoa."

"Whoa, horse," Felicia croaked.

"Like you mean it," the cowboy barked.

"Whoa!" She threw her shoulders back. To her utter amazement, the horse obeyed her and slowed to a rolling gait.

Her rescuer urged his own horse ahead of her, then stopped and dismounted. Felicia pulled back on her horse's mane again. The cowboy stepped forward, his hands raised. The steady cadence of hoofbeats stilled.

The man in the black hat tugged a rope from his rig and slipped it over her horse's neck. "You okay?"

"I'll be fine just as soon as you get me off this four-legged demon." She swung her leg over the animal's neck to sit sidesaddle.

He tipped his head back. The bright moon glinted in his deep pupils as he quirked a cold smile up at her. "I was talking to the horse."

"I don't have time for comedy." She glanced over her shoulder in the direction of her father's ranch, thrusting her arms out to demand help getting down. "I'm in a bit of a hurry."

"I guessed." He crossed his arms over his chest.

Even through the darkness and blue denim, she could tell he had an impressive chest. Lean, hard muscles that came from physical labor, not from hours in the gym and cupboards of health-food concoctions. Todd's over-bulked physique sprang to mind, drawing her back to her immediate dilemma.

"Seriously, sir, I don't have any time to waste."

"Neither do I."

"Good. Then help me down." She spread her arms wider, thinking to place her hands on those broad shoulders.

The smirking smile on his face dropped in an instant. Felicia had no doubt that he'd only now noticed her costume. Cursing the ridiculous situation she'd created, she closed her arms over her torso in a self-conscious gesture.

"That's no bridal gown." His tone bordered on accusatory.

She splayed one hand against the horse's neck to steady herself. The wind sent her long black hair lashing out across her face. Despite that, she managed to glare down at the man. "Bridal gown? Just how much do you know?"

"Not a damned thing about wedding fashions." With a casual flick of his fingers, the man tipped his hat to the back of his head. "But quite a bit about the kind of thing you have on. Though you hardly seem the type to practice the fine art of belly dancing."

Felicia squelched a scream of frustration and clamped one hand to her hips. The gilded chains gracing the top of her harem pants bit into her palm. She took a deep breath. The icy golden coins edging her bra top fell against her warm midriff. Despite the shiver that caused, she aimed her most serene expression at him and said, "This is a disguise, if you must know."

"A disguise?" He snorted with laughter. "I thought the object of wearing a disguise was to make yourself inconspicuous. Honey, that's the last thing you are."

"Perhaps out here." She tossed her head. For an instant, her hair swept from her line of vision. Moonlight fully illuminated the man's face. She gasped as a wave of familiarity engulfed her. Before she could place those rugged features, he yanked his hat brim down over his eyes. She lifted her head and continued, "It just so happens that in a casino in Las Vegas this outfit was the perfect disguise."

"Vegas?" He said it like he'd never heard of the place.

"That's where I've just come from, or rather, where I was taken from." Felicia rolled her eyes and sighed. "It's a long, complicated story, but if you'll help me down I'll try to explain it to you in short, simple words, Mr...."

He reached up, caught her arm and gave it a quick tug. The flimsy fabric of Felicia's outfit slid with ease over the horse's sweat-slick back. Down she went—face first, hurtling toward the hard ground. Her stomach lurched.

She squeezed her eyes shut and prepared for impact. But nothing she could do could have readied her for the jolt she received when her body collided with the cowboy's solid chest.

"Gotcha." His strong arms fastened around her scantily clad body.

Her eyes flew open and locked in an intimate gaze with his. Her nose twitched at the unique scent that clung to him. Woodsmoke and leather. And *him.* Felicia knew she would forever associate the heady masculine aroma with the knee-weakening sensation of this unknown cowboy's embrace. In painfully slow motion, he eased her down, keeping her body pressed to his until her toes touched the ground at last.

"You don't recognize me, do you?" he asked, still holding her closer than she should have allowed.

"Yes, of course I do," Felicia lied. "You're one of my father's ranch hands?"

"The hell I am. But leave it to a mule-headed little brat like you to assume everyone in sight is in your father's pocket." His handsome face hardened and he leaned in to make himself heard above the wind. "Now hear this, Miss High Horse, the only job I'd do for your father is demolition work on that modern palace he's built on my family's land."

"Ethan Bradshaw." If he'd suddenly burst into flames, she couldn't have jumped away from him faster. "What are you doing out here in the middle of nowhere?"

"I'm building a home on the little bit of Bradshaw land your daddy couldn't get his hands on." He jerked his head to indicate the spot where she had almost run over him.

Felicia blinked at the dilapidated trailer gleaming in the moonlight. She angled her shoulders back and folded her arms over her exposed middle. "You're living in a death trap surrounded by nothing but coyotes, snakes and a graveyard, building a home to spite my father, and you call *me* headstrong?"

"Mule-headed," he corrected. "And I'm not doing this to get back at your daddy." A satisfied grin broke over his thin lips. "That's just a happy bonus."

Despite herself, she laughed. If anyone could empathize with that sentiment, it was her. She loved her father, but his domineering presence in her life had driven her to near distraction. She nodded in agreement with Ethan. "I could say the same thing about my marriage to Todd."

"Marriage?" He whisked his black hat off to reveal equally dark hair slicked back over his head and falling into waves at his collar. The stark style brought out his pale blue eyes and emphasized the wicked tilt of his lips as he asked, "When did you get married?"

"Thanks to my father's meddling, I didn't." Her horse shifted and she snatched up the rope tied around its neck.

Ethan took up his horse's reins, as well. He fit his hat back down on his head, then tipped the brim toward the trailer.

"I appreciate the invitation but, I, um, I'm not exactly prepared for walking." She glanced down at her bare feet and Ethan did the same.

To his credit, he only heaved a sigh instead of cussing at her wriggling toes.

"Okay, then." He guided his horse around to her. "Let's go."

She fisted one hand in the wisps of her delicate outfit. "I'm sorry. I left home in a hurry and..."

He blinked at her, showing only mild impatience.

She slid her foot into the stirrup and hoisted herself up onto the horse. When she settled in the saddle, she offered a properly contrite smile. "You may ride my horse, if you'd like."

"Oh, may I?" A laugh rose up from him as he tied the rope restraining her horse to the saddle horn.

"You don't have to get snippy with me."

"Snippy?" He peered up at her. "I've been called a lot of things in my life, lady, but snippy is where I draw the line."

"Sorry to impugn your macho reputation," she said, lowering her lashes over a challenging glare. "I just wanted to give you another option besides walking."

"Mighty democratic of you, Your Highness." He made an exaggerated bow.

Felicia leapt to deny his indictment of her behavior.

He lifted his head. Moonlight flashed over his face and flickered in the depths of his eyes. The words died on her lips. She shuddered at the mixture of disdain and amusement in his expression.

"At the risk of being called something worse than snippy, I have another plan." He reached out and pulled her foot free from the stirrup.

She gasped and clutched the saddle horn. His hand came down over hers. The horse moved sideways. The saddle shifted left. Leather squeaked against leather and denim snagged silk. Felicia shut her eyes as a sudden, unavoidable presence pressed hard against her back. She dared not move for fear of feeling just how intimately Ethan's body molded to hers. Still, the warmth of his body and his arms around her, if only to hold the reins, was welcome.

Ethan clucked softly to his horse and it began to walk slowly back toward the trailer. "Now, suppose you tell me how you came to be barefoot and bareback on a night like this."

The strain in his voice was evident. She drew in her breath, then hesitated. "I have to warn you before I start, this is a pretty crazy mess."

"What else would it be?" His chest rose and fell against her spine. "It involves you."

Felicia chose not to take his baiting and instead dove straight into her tale. "Well, I went to Las Vegas this afternoon planning to elope with my fiancé, Todd Armstrong."

Ethan gripped the reins tighter. "Todd Armstrong, the bodybuilder?"

Felicia twisted to face her companion. "You know him?"

"I did a profile on him for a fitness magazine a couple years back. Interviewed him in the dressing room after he'd won another bodybuilding title." A definite career low point, Ethan thought, but refrained from saying.

"Oh?" She raised one professionally plucked brow. "That hardly sounds like work befitting a Pulitzer Prize winning journalist."

"You know my work?" Maybe Felicia Grantham had more substance than he'd suspected.

She shrugged. "I've seen some of your articles in the type of boring magazines they put in waiting rooms." She crinkled her nose up. "All that news, all those serious subjects, those probing reports. That's just not my usual fare."

So much for substance. Ethan adjusted in the saddle to put a centimeter more space between himself and her nearly perfect body. "Sorry I never did anything you could appreciate."

"Oh, I don't know. You did a story on my fiancé. I hope you didn't find it too intimidating, asking him questions while he stood there in a tiny swimsuit, his magnificent muscles oiled and bulging." She looked back at him, mischief flashing in her eyes and her full lips tilting at a playful angle.

Ethan huffed.

"What else could interest a girl like me, after all?" she asked in a breathy, pouting tone. She stuck her finger in her flowing hair and twirled one ebony strand. "That depressing stuff, like your piece on homeless children, gives me a headache."

She'd played him for a fool—and damned if he didn't admire the woman for it. Ethan chuckled. "Okay, so you're not just some silly little airhead. You could have just said you knew my work in the first place."

"And pass up the chance to take Ethan Bradshaw down a notch?" She laughed. "Not likely."

They reached the trailer and Ethan cocked his head to study her profile. "Is someone going to come looking for you anytime soon?"

Felicia shook her head. "I paid the stable hand to lead my father and my bodyguard on a merry chase. Until they catch up with him, they'll assume it was me tearing out in the ranch pickup."

Ethan nodded, unsure of what else to say. Felicia shifted restlessly. A soft clinking drew his attention to the glittering coins on her bra top. He glanced down over her shoulder, then caught his breath.

Moonlight created a liquid glow over the rich tawny skin that told of Felicia Grantham's Hispanic heritage. That shimmering light highlighted the roundness of her breasts in their brief covering. Ethan shifted in his tightening jeans. Suddenly aware of her bottom nestled to his lap, he jumped to get down from the horse. He helped her down in short order.

She murmured a thank-you, then stood there, her huge eyes fixed on his face.

Say something, you idiot, his brain urged. "I have to admit, it's not my usual style to deal with half-naked people."

Felicia snatched at one of the scarves clinging to her hair. She drew it over one shoulder, folding her arms to secure the translucent streamer over her exposed skin. "Well, I'm sorry if my appearance offends you."

"Your appearance?" Ethan blinked. "Oh." He snorted a telling laugh. "You thought I meant..." He waved his hand at her getup. "Trust me, honey, your appearance does a lot of things, but offending me isn't one of them."

Her arms relaxed beneath her breasts.

"The remark about half-naked people was a reference to my piece on Todd Armstrong. It was my lame attempt at getting the conversation back on him." He stole the reins from her hands and tied both horses to a scrubby bush beside the trailer.

"Todd?" She shook her head, paused, then tossed back her glossy black curls. "You mean my teasing about his muscles?"

"My ego insists I let you know I only did that fitness article as a favor to a..." He coughed into his fist, then opened his hand to shrug off his conclusion. "A friend."

A light, lyrical laugh answered him. Felicia nodded and extended her arms with a flourish. "Say no more. I thoroughly understand the lengths one will go to for..."

Love. Ethan's mind completed the thought before Felicia voiced it. But lust, not love, for a pretty story editor had motivated him. He pressed his lips together, ready to set her straight. Before he could accomplish that, she summed up her own statement.

"A member of the opposite sex," she said with a sigh.

The vague reference pricked at Ethan's naturally suspicious mind, as did her bland tone. What was Miss High Horse up to? Was she following true love or was there another explanation for her shenanigans? "Suppose we go inside and you can tell me the whole sordid story."

Ethan showed her to the front door of the trailer. For a moment, he doubted if she would accept his hospitality. Then she heaved a sigh of resignation and climbed inside. He joined her, flipping the dim overhead light on before pulling the door shut with a sturdy thud.

"My, isn't this cozy?" She glanced over her shoulder.

"Damned cozy," he croaked out. The cramped quarters kept her kissably close. "Sorry it isn't what you're used to."

"I wasn't complaining," she whispered.

Outside, the wind howled, blasting against the old trailer until it shuddered. Felicia gasped. Ethan dipped his chin. Their gazes tangled in wary regard. A smile trembled on her inviting lips.

With one hand, he pulled off his hat and flung it onto the faded red countertop. He filled his lungs with the jumble of scents from the enclosed space. The yellowed cedar of the cupboards. The dusty twenty-year-old curtains. The almost irresistible woman standing just inches away from him.

He imagined closing the distance between them, putting his hands on her shoulders. She would tip her head back. Soft ebony waves of hair would bounce over his fingers.

His gaze fell on her waiting mouth. Wind rocked the trailer in a gentle, seductive rhythm. Ethan wondered what she would do if he acted on his impulse.

Suddenly, two bright circles of light sliced across the mobile home, followed by the quiet purr of an expensive automobile approaching on the nearby road.

Felicia tensed. "That has to be my father," she whispered. "He must know by now that I wasn't in the truck and he's come back to look for me."

Her dark eyes flared wide with anxious anticipation. She staggered backward until the edge of the small pedestal table met her bottom. She braced herself straight-armed and held her breath. Ethan twisted his head to peer over his shoulder through the window. The headlights flashed in his eyes as the car made the curve. Then it sped past.

Felicia slumped back. "I guess he never dreamed I'd pick this place as a hideout."

"So, you're safe for a while longer. Why don't you use the time to tell me just how you got into this mess? Then maybe we can think of a way to get you out of it."

She tilted her head to one side. "Why, Ethan Bradshaw, I think you mean it."

"Sit." He stabbed one finger at the red vinyl breakfast bench behind the table. She obeyed. "Before we get started, can I get you anything?"

She glanced down, then smiled sheepishly up at him. "A shirt would be nice."

Ethan gave her a curt nod, turned and disappeared through a narrow, curtained archway. The whole trailer shook under his footsteps. After all these years, she still found Ethan Bradshaw indescribably sexy. Why hadn't the sting of his cruel rejection of her tender affection or the passing of time dulled his impact on her?

Something peculiar fluttered in her stomach and the image of Ethan Bradshaw's mouth on hers sprang into her mind. His arms circled her body, pulling her closer and closer. She fisted her hand in the silky fabric skimming over her thigh and sank her teeth into her lower lip.

"Here you go." Ethan tossed a large red-and-black-flannel shirt onto her lap.

She jumped a foot.

"Sorry. Daydreaming about Loverboy?" he asked with a hint of irritation.

"Actually, I was—" She caught herself before she confessed anything embarrassing. In a few quick movements, she slid the oversize shirt over her shoulders. "I was just recounting the evening's events in my mind." She shook her head. "I guess I'm a little distracted."

He leaned back against the kitchen counter. "It's been a night full of distractions, I'd say."

"But things have settled down now." She cast him a quick glance under her lowered lashes.

Ethan crossed his arms over his chest.

"Anyway..." She wrapped the huge shirt around her slender body, reveling in the comfort of it. The nubby fabric of the collar rubbed against her cheek and she sighed in contentment. "I suppose I owe you an explanation."

"I'm listening."

"Well, it all started when I met Todd at a party for charity."

"Don't tell me, it was love at first sight." Ethan rolled his eyes heavenward.

"Spoken like a dyed-in-the-wool skeptic," she shot back. "If you must know, it wasn't love at first sight, or second sight or..." She stiffened. "Or anything that simple. Todd Armstrong is a very persistent man who goes after the things he wants. Over the last two months he won me over. Last week he proposed."

"Two months? That's all the time you've known this clown?"

"Are you going to stand there making sarcastic commentary like... like..." She wanted a comparison to gall the arrogant jerk into silence. "Like my father," she concluded triumphantly. "Or will you let me finish?"

He glowered at her, his mouth sealed in an unwavering line.

"Thank you." She bowed her head in quick concession. "Last week, we devised a plan to meet in Las Vegas at a hotel where Todd was judging a bodybuilding contest. From there, we had only a short drive to a wedding chapel and then straight on to happily ever after."

She lifted her gaze to his face, challenging him to make another remark. His lips twitched but did not open. She held her hands out and shrugged. "Well, my father got wind of the plan and arrived at the casino just as we were leaving."

"That's when he hauled your little butt back here?"

"No, that's when I pulled some strings with the casino owner and bought this costume." She reached beneath the unbuttoned shirt to pinch the strap of her white top. "They have an Arabian Nights theme."

"That's how you managed to blend in with the crowd, then."

"It would have worked, too, if Todd and I hadn't gone to the chapel in separate cars. I floored it all the way, thinking we'd get there in time to have a quick ceremony before my father could intervene. Todd, on the other hand, must have obeyed every speed limit and yellow light. He drove up just seconds ahead of my father. Dad started bellowing and suddenly Todd forgot all his respect for traffic laws. He tore out of there as fast as his candy-apple-red convertible could take him."

"Little coward," Ethan mumbled. "And you were going to marry him."

"Going to? I still am."

"You're kidding."

"I'm serious."

"But why?"

"That isn't something a man like you could understand."

Ethan choked out a bitter laugh. "You may have a point, there, Miss High Horse."

"Don't call me that," she snapped. She folded herself tightly into the buffalo plaid shirt. "My motives aren't really relevant now, anyway. The important thing is getting me back to Vegas and my fiancé."

"What makes you so sure that your muscle man will still be there?"

"Because he lives there, smarty."

"Sounds appropriate." Ethan smoothed his hand back over his hair. "Big phony like Armstrong would choose to live in a place that's all surface glitter like Vegas."

"I could care less what you think of my fiancé, Bradshaw. What I want to know is, will you help me get back to him?"

He scowled at her.

"I'll pay you handsomely."

"Oh, no you won't." Ethan straightened away from the counter. He clamped his large hands on his lean hips. His blue eyes practically sparked with indignation. "Maybe that tactic works with the stable hand or the casino manager, but nothing about me is for sale, lady. Not my time, not my effort and certainly not my compassion."

"I...I didn't mean to insult you." She swallowed hard. Suddenly, Ethan's shirt chafed the back of her neck, her arms, her midriff—everywhere it touched her bare skin.

"I'm sorry to have bothered you with all this." She peeled the shirt from her body and swung her legs from beneath the table. "Thank you for helping me with my horse."

She stood and took a single step toward the door when his hand captured her arm. "Where are you going?"

Felicia looked up into his puzzled face and tipped her chin up. "I'm going to Las Vegas. And if you won't help me..."

He muttered something under his breath as he retrieved the flannel shirt she'd dropped on the table. He held it out to her. "I said I wasn't for sale. That doesn't mean I won't help you."

"But why would you?" She accepted the shirt.

"I have my reasons. And like you said, the rest is irrelevant."

"You're doing it to get back at my father, aren't you? If you get me to Todd, then he'll look like a big old fool."

Ethan just smiled.

"Well, all right. It's a deal." She thrust out her hand to him.

He glanced down but kept his hands firmly on his hips. "Not so fast. Before I agree to be seen traipsing over the countryside with a belly-dancer bride, I'm going to have to insist on one condition."

Felicia wet her lips. "I don't like ultimatums, Bradshaw."

Ethan shrugged. "You don't have to like it, Grantham. But if you even hope to pull this off, you'll have to agree to my terms."

Chapter Two

A camera strobe flashed in the dim light of dawn, causing the two horses to nicker and shy.

"Stop that," Felicia hissed, swatting Ethan's intrusive camera lens away.

"Hey, you agreed to the terms, lady—exclusive rights to chronicle every twist of your maniacal misadventures in exchange for reuniting you with Loverboy." Ethan readjusted the focus on his intimidating-looking camera. Almost-inaudible clicks and whirs punctuated his snide remarks. "The story just wouldn't be complete without a shot of you, dressed in my clothes, sneaking into your own father's stable."

A second explosion of light burst before Felicia's eyes, blinding her. The horses shuffled and snorted in response behind her. She thrust her hand out until her palm made contact with the rim of the camera lens. She gave it a firm shove. "The story won't ever have the chance to be complete if we get caught at this stage of the game."

"It's six in the morning. Who's going to catch us?"

The dark blur before her eyes faded into the image of Ethan standing with his hands on his hips, his gaze hard as flint on her face.

"We made a deal, Bradshaw. If you want out..." She took a deep breath to still her nerves. Her pulse sped. To her relief, pride was able to hold her tears of frustration at bay long enough for her to point one finger toward the barn door. "Then get on your horse and ride."

The hollow in his tanned cheek ticked. His lips twitched in a cold half smile. His horse pawed the ground. Ethan shifted his weight like a fighter taking a stance.

She jerked her chin up high. "But if you intend to honor your word..."

He scowled at the implication he would do otherwise. "Then I suggest you do things my way. That means no more pictures until we're safely on our way."

"Yes, ma'am." He tipped the brim of his hat toward her. "Whatever you say."

Oozing confidence, she turned her back.

"Miss High Horse."

She spun on her heel. "Don't you dare call me that again, Bradshaw."

He laughed.

Felicia cursed herself for letting him reduce her to a childish temper fit. She narrowed her eyes in warning. The pungent aroma of hay and horses filled the electrified air between them.

"I've known since I was sixteen what you thought of me, Bradshaw. You don't have to remind me," she heard herself say in a deceptively calm tone. "But let me remind you of something—by giving you this story and photo-op, I'm providing you with some pretty sweet revenge on my father."

"You have your own motives for doing this, sister. So don't try manipulating me through guilt," he said.

"Fine." She snapped her head up. "But I expect the same courtesy from you." She led the black horse into its stall.

"Me?" He followed her with his own horse on his heels. "I never used guilt to—"

"Oh, please!" She whipped around and found her nose practically buried in his chest. With both hands flattened to his denim jacket, she gave him a respectable push. He staggered back a step and she moved forward. "If I have to hear one more word about how my father robbed your father out of his precious family land, I'll..."

"What?" Ethan demanded, standing firm.

He had her there. Her current situation hardly gave her any room for threats. She huffed and pushed past him. "Put your horse in the next stall."

Ethan complied. When he'd taken care of his horse, he came out of the stall to discover her standing in a shaft of light from the open barn door. The rising sun cast a glow over her high cheekbones and haloed the crown of her hair. But the long mane that tumbled down her back seemed to absorb every glimmer of light that touched it. The image only reinforced her reference to their brief encounter when she was just sixteen. For an instant he longed to do now what he dared not then.

His fingers flexed at the notion of tangling his hands in that hair. Of tipping her head back. Of kissing those plump, pouty lips. He grit his teeth and held his breath. She was still extraordinary.

She turned to face him. "Are you going to stand there all day gawking, Bradshaw, or can we get moving?"

Yeah, an extraordinary pain in the rear. With all these memories flashing through his head, how could that little detail have slipped his mind? Lucky for him, if he ever forgot it again, he'd only have to wait a second or two and she'd open her mouth. One word from Her Highness was enough to dissuade any man of his romantic fantasies.

"Let's get this show on the road," he said, striding up to her. "The sooner I get you to your destination, the sooner I get my new life back on track."

"Good." She bent to gather up something at her feet. "While you stabled your horse, I retrieved my purse from where I stashed it last night."

"Looks like you also found some cowboy boots to wear."

"I scrounged them up from the tack room." She pushed at the shirt cuffs hanging past her wrists, then tugged up the elastic band at the top of the sweatpants he'd loaned her, thrusting one foot toward him. "They're a little big but they get the job done, wouldn't you say?"

"Very chic." He shook his head at her ridiculous get-up. "Maybe you'll start a trend."

She struck a pose. "I call it aerobic-cowboy-grunge. What do you think?"

"I think I'll never figure you out." He reached the barn door and grabbed the rough wooden frame with one hand. The dawn warmed her features as he peered down into her face. "One minute you act like the queen of everything, the next you poke fun at yourself." He curled one finger beneath her chin. "Which one is the real Felicia Grantham?"

"Uh-uh, Bradshaw." She wrenched her head away, shaking her hair over her hunched shoulders. "Self-revelation is not part of our bargain."

She pivoted on the worn heel of her oversize cowboy boot and flounced outside. Ethan watched her go, struck with the thought that he might be the one who ended up paying for the so-called revenge he hoped to exact.

Ethan shoved his new Stetson down on his head, allowing time for Felicia to get into his Blazer. She'd driven it over while he'd brought the horses. Too bad they couldn't make the whole trip with such safe distance between them. He secured the barn door behind him and made his way to the vehicle. He slid into the driver's seat, smirked and asked, "Making yourself pretty for me?"

Felicia dropped the small makeup mirror into the red purse in her lap. "Just assessing the damage, Bradshaw. I'd hate to look so bad that I drew too much attention to myself."

"You?" He jabbed the key into the ignition and started the engine. "Shunning attention? That'll be the day."

"I didn't say I was shunning all attention," she replied coolly. "Just negative attention. Nothing would spoil our freedom run like small children shrieking in terror and pointing at my streaked mascara and frazzled hair."

There it was again—the unexpected answer. Where was the fire and fury he'd expected? Ethan glanced over at her. A smile curved on her full lips. Damn it, if she kept this up, he just might be tempted to act on his long-smoldering attraction to her. Then what? He pushed his foot down fully on the gas pedal and the truck lunged forward.

"Cool it, will you?" Felicia lurched sideways, her arm straight out to him. "Gun that engine again and you'll wake the whole house. Our goal is to get away undetected."

"I know our goal." He eased up on the gas and guided the truck down the long drive that led to the road.

"Then kindly act like it." She clicked her tongue.

"Listen, woman..." He turned onto the main road. "You talk to me like that again and—"

"Like what?" She batted her thick lashes at him in surprised innocence.

"Like you were giving orders to a servant."

"Oh, that's silly." She waved a hand in the air, shifting in the seat to put her profile to him. "You're not a servant."

"Darn right," he muttered.

"You're more like contract labor."

"What?"

"Watch the road," she cried as the truck swerved.

Ethan manhandled the steering wheel, secretly wishing it was a certain young lady's lovely neck. "Personally, I like to think of myself as your noble protector, coming to your rescue in your hour of need in my blue Blazer."

"Well, don't you have an active imagination?" She rolled her dark eyes heavenward. "I, on the other hand, realize that people can only rescue themselves. Which is what I have done."

"You have?" He gave her a calculated laugh.

"Indeed I have." She angled her shoulders away from him, gazing from the window as if the dry, flat land were the most interesting landscape in the world. "I made a deal with you, Bradshaw. I didn't trick you into helping me. And I for darn sure didn't beg you to rescue me like some damsel in distress."

"No, I guess you didn't." Suddenly, Ethan noticed how the windshield magnified the intensity of the morning sun. He reached out to flick on the air conditioner. A stale, lukewarm blast answered his action. "Still, you have to admit, I'm a little more involved than a hired hand. After all, I'm incurring the wrath of a very powerful man in order to earn you some independence."

"No, that's Todd's job," she said softly.

"I beg your pardon?" Had she just made some kind of confession or had he taken her murmurings too literally? His mind raced at the possibilities. The journalist saw a new angle for his story. But deeper still, he felt honest concern.

He flicked his hat back with one finger and studied her. What drastic measures could she be taking in order to break away from her domineering father? "Felicia? Is there something you want to tell me about this whirlwind marriage to Todd Armstrong?"

"I told you the whole story last night, Bradshaw." Her dark brows clashed down in angry slashes over her stormy eyes. "I don't owe you another word. Just do your part and I'll live up to my end of our bargain."

Cold air blew from the open vents along the dashboard. Ethan straightened. He fixed his gaze on the endless line of the road ahead. "Whatever you say."

Felicia lay her head against the window, closing her eyes to shut out Ethan's encroaching presence. She had no idea how much time had passed when a sudden jostling awakened her.

"Oh, my." A yawn welled up from deep within her. "I didn't intend to take a nap. Was I out long?"

Ethan shrugged. "Almost an hour."

She blinked to force the sleep from her eyes. As the bleariness cleared, the outskirts of a small town came into view on the horizon. "Oh, good. This looks like the perfect place to take a break."

"Bad idea. We need to get some miles behind us."

"And I need to get some food inside me," she argued. "I haven't eaten since yesterday noon."

"We'll pick up some chips and soda at a gas station on our way out of town, then."

"Chips? Soda?" She pressed her palm over her empty stomach. "How do you expect me to survive on that? I need a meal."

"Maybe a little lobster bisque? Fresh-baked bread? Grilled salmon steak?" he asked in a low, almost seductive voice.

"Mmm." Felicia shut her eyes and inhaled, half expecting to smell the rich aroma of the food. Her stomach growled in anticipation. "Sounds heavenly."

"Maybe you haven't noticed, but we're nowhere near heaven." He reduced speed as they approached the city limits sign.

"Smokewater, Texas, Population 1008," Felicia read.

"You'll be lucky if you can get anything better than a couple of greasy eggs or a day-old doughnut in this place."

"I'll take it." She sat up and began to smooth down her hair. "That looks like a diner up ahead—let's eat there."

Ethan halted at a wide-open four-way stop. To their left, a large tractor hauling some type of farm equipment chugged to life and began to roll slowly through the intersection.

"You do plan on stopping at the diner, don't you, Ethan?"

He gave a curt nod to the man on the tractor but made no response to her question.

"Spare me your strong, silent-type routine, Bradshaw." Her breath came in angry huffs. "I'm in charge here and say we stop."

"You're in charge?" He scowled at her from beneath the brim of his black hat. "Since when?"

She narrowed one eye at him like a gunman taking aim down a rifle barrel. "Since always."

He dismissed her threatening tone with a sputtering chuckle. "Maybe you haven't noticed, but I'm the one in the driver's seat."

"And I can boot you right out of it anytime I have to."

"Yeah?"

"Yeah."

"Let's see you try." He squinted at her with one eye shut.

The look set a tremor off in her being that turned her insides to molten liquid. It also brought her to a monumentous conclusion. Never in a million years was she going to outstubborn Ethan Bradshaw—any more than she could outstubborn a mule.

No, the way to budge this immovable object, she decided, was with finesse, not force. She had to stop thinking of him as being made of granite and start seeing him as a fly to be caught in a clever spider's web.

Beyond them, the tractor coughed and spewed a cloud of gray smoke into the clean morning air. It had almost cleared the road. She had to act fast.

Arranging her face in an expression of gracious resignation, she sighed. "You're right, Ethan. You are in the driver's seat and it's your call whether we stop at the café or not."

Ethan flinched.

She wanted to ask him if he'd been bitten by something—a spider, maybe—but she refrained.

The hollow of Ethan's tanned cheeks reddened. Seething accusation burned in his eyes. "Cut that out."

"Cut what out?" She held her hands out and shrugged.

"You know what," he shot back. "You're being nice and I don't trust it."

She laughed in earnest. "Nice? How nice can I be? I'm willing to let you lose a terrific photo opportunity to your own willful arrogance."

He wrapped his hands around the steering wheel and glared straight ahead. Felicia watched her poisoned provocation take effect. His jaw thrust forward. His knuckles turned white.

The tractor and its load made it through the intersection. The farmer waved, then dropped his gloved hand to the gearshift. The old gears groaned. The filthy tractor belched out another puff of smoke.

"You can go now." Felicia offered him a saccharine smile.

"Not until you explain that last remark."

"About the photo opportunity?" She batted her lashes at him and cocked her head.

"Yes," he said through clenched teeth.

And the spider snares the unsuspecting fly, she thought. "Well, I can't help thinking..."

He fit his hand over the crown of his hat and dipped the brim forward. "Yes?"

"You wanted to chronicle my every movement on my way back to Todd." She focused her gaze ahead and gave a quick nod toward the small diner. "Can you honestly imagine a better picture for your story than Gower Grantham's daughter eating in a small-town greasy spoon?"

A smile crept over Ethan's hard lips....

Ten minutes later, they had placed their orders.

"How long before our food is ready?" Felicia asked the waitress when she paused to fill their coffee cups.

The rail-thin woman stood back and gave her customers the once-over. Holding the coffeepot at shoulder height, she tugged a pad from the pocket of her muslin apron and glanced down at the order she had just taken. Her angular hips shifted in her brown Western pants as she cocked her head and considered. "Oh, twenty minutes, give or take. There a problem with that, miss?"

"No, no problem." Felicia shook her head. "That will be all, thank you."

The waitress turned, her head bobbing as she mimicked Felicia's dismissal in silence. When she had her backside to him, the woman twisted her head to peer over her shoulder at Ethan. "How 'bout you, honey? You need anything else?"

He plopped his hat onto the seat beside him and leaned forward. In his best cowboy drawl he said, "As a matter of fact, I do, darlin'."

The waitress lowered her obviously false eyelashes at him and wet her thickly glossed lips. "What can I do you for?"

Ethan grinned at the expression, thinking how nice it was to be home in Texas. He might have continued the harmless flirtation if he hadn't sensed a chill as subtle as a blue norther from across the table. He pressed his shoulders back against the tattered café bench. "I wonder if I could get you to pose for a picture or two for me?"

"Aw, c'mon." The woman turned and shook her head at him. "I may have been born at night, mister, but it wasn't *last night.*"

"You can say that again," Felicia mumbled to the ceiling.

The waitress snarled at Felicia, then focused her gaze on Ethan. "Even out here in Smokewater we've heard about the old photographer's model scam. And if you think you can get me out of my clothes that easy, you've got—"

Ethan grinned up at her in his most disarming manner. "No, no, darlin', you've got me all wrong. I'm a reporter doing a story on the demise of the small-town diner. I just want a few photos of you and my assistant to go with the article."

She squinted warily at the camera he held up.

"All I want is a picture or two of you waiting on Miss High Horse, here." He stabbed two fingers in Felicia's direction, knowing the gesture, coupled with the nickname, would irk her just as surely as if he had actually poked her in the ribs.

Felicia crossed her arms and glowered at him, totally unaware that her display of pure irritation probably clinched the waitress's decision.

"Okay," the woman said. She raised her hand to the teased bubble of curls atop her head. The pearly pink polish on her eye-catching plastic nails contrasted with her wine-red hair. "What do I have to do?"

Ethan grinned and quickly arranged the two subjects before either could back out. After a few minutes, he had his shots and the waitress had scurried off to give their order to the cook.

"Now that that nonsense is over..." Felicia scooted to the end of her seat, then swung her legs out into the aisle. "I'm going to make use of the next twenty minutes to get myself into some decent clothing."

"What the blazes are you talking about?" Ethan swept his open palm over his black hair to smooth it in place.

She nodded toward the street framed by the café's picture window. "I can see a shop owner opening up a little store across the way. I'm going to pop in and pick up a few things."

"Sit down." He shook his head. "We don't have the time to cater to your vanity now."

"My vanity?" Thick, grease-laced air rushed into her lungs through her gaping mouth. A thousand blistering insults tangled in her mind.

Out of the corner of her eye, she saw Ethan reach for his camera.

She'd suspected she looked atrocious before, but she felt certain her appearance was nothing short of monstrous now. In an act of self-preservation, she snatched up her purse and whipped away from him. "I'll be back in twenty minutes."

"Suit yourself," Ethan called out after her. "But I'm leaving as soon as I finish my breakfast—with or without you."

Leave without her? Felicia's boots scuffed over the dirty diner's floor. *Preposterous.* She strode outside and across the street. *He wouldn't.* She pressed her palm to the brass plate on the store's front door. *He couldn't.* The cold metal stung her hand. *Could he?* She gasped and threw an anxious look over her shoulder at the diner where she'd left Ethan. *Don't be silly.* She pushed her way inside the store, laughing softly. *Only a complete and total jerk would leave a woman stranded in the middle of nowhere.*

Chapter Three

"Only a complete and total jerk would leave a woman stranded in the middle of nowhere," Ethan muttered to himself through clenched teeth. He stomped his boot down on the brake and brought his truck to a halt in a cloud of dust. A quick glance in his rearview mirror brought the distant outline of the small town into sight.

He groaned a curse for Felicia Grantham and what she'd reduced him to: a journalistic mercenary who could barely contain his temper or his libido. What had ever possessed him to get involved with that woman anyway? He should be home right now, clearing a patch of land for his home like the newly settled, retired person that he was.

Settled? Retired? The words galled him even as they entered his mind. He huffed another curse and gripped the steering wheel. Why he'd taken on Felicia's cause wasn't important, he realized in that instant. He'd done it and Ethan Bradshaw wasn't the kind of man who left a job half-done just because it became disagreeable. He hadn't gotten that soft—not yet.

He twisted the wheel hard to the right and accelerated. If he pushed it, he could be back in town before Felicia's fury reached the absolute boiling point.

Felicia crossed her arms over her pink T-shirt. She tapped her white canvas tennis shoe on the pavement, causing the stiff leg of her new jeans to brush the bag containing her old clothes. The morning sun glared high in the sky. She shielded her eyes and squinted around the corner of the town's crossroads. Nothing.

"Where is he?" she whispered, scanning the deserted streets. He's gone, her mind taunted. And he's not coming back.

She shut her eyes. What was she going to do now? Panic fluttered in her chest. Deep in her stomach the first stirrings of fear created a cold, clammy sensation.

Images from the past twenty minutes fit together in her mind like a disquieting crazy quilt. It all began in the café with Ethan. That, followed by a scene in the little store when the clerk had been unable to accept a credit card, forcing Felicia to dip into her cash reserve to pay for her dowdy new clothes.

So, she'd been in a pretty testy mood when she'd returned to the diner and found Ethan gone. Yet she'd rallied. She knew herself to be a resourceful woman capable of handling any setback between herself and her quest for personal freedom. With one quick scan of the room, she'd found a likely substitute for Ethan Bradshaw and marched right up to him. A deal was struck. She handed him five hundred of her remaining six hundred dollars then plunked herself down to eat her cold breakfast while he gassed up his truck for the journey.

What had she been thinking? she wondered. Giving almost every cent she had to a total stranger? But what choice had she had? Once Ethan Bradshaw had bailed out on her, she had to find another way to Las Vegas. She puffed out a hard chuckle at her own bravado. How could she have thought that a man like Ethan would remain at her beck and call? And then, how could she have believed the best way to resolve her self-inflicted dilemma was by paying some coffee-swilling good ol' boy to haul her to Vegas like so much freight?

She shook her head and opened her eyes, hoping against hope to see her ride materialize on the empty street.

"Hey, lady, need a lift?" Ethan leaned out the window of his dusty blue Blazer as he pulled to stop in front of her.

Unadulterated relief swept over her. For an instant, she wallowed in it. "It scalds my tongue to say this, Bradshaw, but you're a welcome sight."

He cut the engine and stepped out onto the street. The sun glowed golden along the low-slanted rim of his Stetson and he flashed a cocky grin. "Sounds like this time on your own has made you appreciate me." He cupped his hands over her shoulders and bent his head to peer at her, eye level. "Can't say I'm surprised, though. I figured you would succumb to my charm eventually—even if I did have to teach you a lesson first."

She hooked her thumbs in her belt loops and fortified her stance. "Teach me a lesson?"

"Now, don't be embarrassed to admit your defeat, Miss High Horse. You were outgunned the minute you tried to take on the master." He poked his thumb into his own expanded chest. "It was only a matter of time until you came around."

"Come around?" Hot, acidic pride welled up in Felicia's throat, singeing her words. She tossed her head to throw her windblown hair off her face. "I'm right where you left me, Bradshaw. You're the one who seems to be coming around."

He raised one eyebrow in questioning challenge.

"My guess is it's unfinished business that brought you back to Smokewater, not the scenery."

"That's right," Ethan growled, dropping his hand from her shoulder. He moved back to the truck and pulled open the passenger door. "I came back because I realized I owed you something."

"I thought so."

"This." He reached behind the seat to yank free a dark green duffel bag. Without further warning, he threw it into her midsection.

Felicia caught the lightweight bag just as it grazed her stomach. Ethan hadn't tossed it hard enough to hurt anything but her pride. She fumbled with the seeming evidence that he had not really returned for her. She managed to loosen the drawstring top to peek inside.

"Oh, for..." She let go of the olive drab duffel. The pliant canvas bag hit the sidewalk with a muffled thud followed by the clank of its brass fixtures. "Like I could possibly believe that you drove back here just to return my belly dancer's costume."

Ethan cocked a mischievous grin. "Well, you never know when a thing like that might come in handy."

"Oh, please." She rolled her eyes. "Why is it so hard for you to admit that I'm the reason you came back?"

"Maybe it's the same reason you can't admit that you *need* my help."

She clenched her teeth and stared at him in stony silence.

"See what I mean?" He sighed, then shook his head. "Well, despite that greasy café breakfast, I still have one artery that isn't completely blocked." He stepped up on the curb and nodded toward the dingy diner. "When you're ready to climb down off your high horse and ask for my help again, I'll be inside, working toward my first heart attack."

"And you can just wait there until you have that heart attack, for all I care, Bradshaw."

Ethan's broad shoulders lifted then fell in a tight but casual shrug. "And I suppose that means Todd Armstrong can just wait that long for you, too?"

"He won't have to." She narrowed her eyes and gloried in a snooty shake of her head. "I expect to be in Las Vegas and in Todd's arms on schedule."

Ethan froze in his tracks. He paused. Then, slowly, as if fighting his own better judgment, he twisted only his head to glare at her from the corner of one eye. "How?"

Felicia swallowed. Good sense told her not to propagate the lie, that it could only bring more trouble. But somehow Ethan Bradshaw's presence awakened a beast inside her that gobbled up every last ounce of reason she possessed. Provoking him by any means necessary became her utmost goal.

She crossed her arms and fixed a sweet but smug smile on her face. "What did you think, Bradshaw? That you're the only man in Texas who owns a truck capable of transporting a lady to Las Vegas?"

Bursts of deep red scorched the hollow of his lean cheek. His huge hands flexed into tight fists at his sides. All color drained from his tightly drawn lips. When he spoke, his voice rumbled like thunder warning of an impending storm. "What the devil have you been up to while I was gone, Felicia?"

Sweet satisfaction at his reaction buoyed her confidence. She poked her nose high in the swift breeze and batted her lashes at him. "I've simply done what any self-reliant person might do. I've hired another driver."

"Oh?" His chest heaved as he walked the few feet back to her. "And who might this other driver be?"

She dropped her nose down a notch. Her batting lashes reverted to rapid blinking as she wracked her brain. "Um, Drake," she finally blurted out with a falsely cheery tone. "R-Rob...no, Rod. Rod Drake."

"Rod Drake?" His voice was so quiet, she scarcely heard it. "That's it? That's all you know about the man you intend to go off with down miles of deserted road?"

"Of course not." She pushed a tangle of black hair back from her heat-tinged cheeks. "I asked for references, which he gave. And the men in the diner said he was okay."

"The men in the diner said he was okay," Ethan parroted in deadpan.

"Well, what was I supposed to do? You left me stranded." She stabbed a finger into his hard chest. "And desperate situations call for desperate measures."

Ethan dropped his gaze to the place where her finger remained pressed into his breastbone. "So, where is he now, this desperate man you've hired?"

Felicia dropped her hand. "He'll be here."

Ethan crossed his arms. "Mind if I wait around? Ask him a few questions?"

"Yes, I do mind." *Stop lying,* her last thread of common sense screamed. *You're painting yourself into a corner.*

Ethan studied her, his gorgeous face the incarnation of patronizing concern.

"I mind very much. You have been replaced, Bradshaw. Accept it and hit the road." *Why settle for painting yourself into a corner when you can wall yourself up inside a tomb?* "My new ride will be here any minute."

"Fine." Ethan walked over to the diner, situated his back against the chipped stucco facade, adjusted his hat and crossed his arms.

"What do you think you're doing?" She planted her fists on her hips.

"Waiting for a train." He kicked one leg out and crossed it over the other at the ankles.

"Very funny." She bent to gather the duffel and shopping bag at her feet, pivoted and marched to the curb. On tiptoe, she leaned out to scan the lonely crossroads once again. Not even a dog was on the streets. She drew in her breath to sigh, remembered her audience of one, then used the excess air to whistle a wispy tune.

Behind her, Ethan coughed out a scornful laugh. She jerked her spine stiff, feeling his gaze on her like fingers pressing into the rigid muscles of her back. The sensation was at once both irritating and erotic. Neither of which helped her cope with the circumstances.

She shimmied her shoulders as if that could shake away Ethan's watchful presence, but it clung to her like a damp film over her heated skin. She shifted her weight. Her starchy jeans rasped. She folded her arms over the soft jersey material of her new T-shirt. Ethan's gaze remained plastered to her.

This had to stop. If Ethan wanted a showdown in Smokewater then she'd give him one he wouldn't easily forget. She spun on her heel and marched straight for the arrogant creep. "Okay. I blew it, Bradshaw," she heaved at top volume. "This Drake character took off with five hundred dollars of my money in his pocket and he is not coming back."

Ethan stood tall, blinked at her and let his arms fall away from their knot over his chest.

"I know it. And you know it." She threw the bag and duffel onto the pavement. The action lightened her load physically and symbolically. "Probably every person in that diner knows it."

The rounded toes of her sneakers bumped the pointed tips of Ethan's cowboy boots. His eyebrows lifted in surprise at her aggression. But she wasn't finished yet. To bring herself closer, she leaned in. Her upturned chin brushed the fabric of his shirt. "I was on my own for less than half an hour and I made a royal mess of things."

She straightened away and huffed out a relieved sigh. "There. I said it—before you could, I might add. Are you happy?"

He opened his mouth and shook his head.

"Why don't you grab your nasty little camera and take a picture now?" she jeered, tossing her hair back in defiance. "You can caption it Miss High Horse Gets her Comeuppance."

"My aim in chronicling your flight was to humiliate your father, Felicia, not you," Ethan said so softly that she wondered for a moment if she'd only imagined it.

He pushed past her and headed for his Blazer. When he reached it, he popped open the passenger door, turned and motioned to offer the seat to her.

"That's it?" Felicia extended her arms out, palms up at her sides. "No jokes at my expense? No 'I told you so'? No more 'my way or the highway' lectures?"

"That's it." He jerked his head toward the empty cab. "Now, I'm going to Vegas. You with me?"

For the first time since this whole one-woman circus began, Felicia had no comeback. She couldn't even look him in the eye. She simply stood there, her shoulders slumped forward, and nodded to him. The sight touched Ethan more than he should have let it. What did he care if Felicia had been humbled? Wasn't she long overdue for it? And didn't it make his job a damn sight easier? Still, when she lumbered toward him with resignation in her eyes, he couldn't help himself.

"Oh, Felicia," he said just as she stepped one foot inside the Blazer.

Her head snapped up. Their eyes met.

"There is one thing I have to say before we get going again."

"What?"

"If you ever pull another stunt like this..."

His implied threat seemed to infuse her posture with renewed vigor. Sparks danced in the depths of her eyes but she held her tongue.

He was a fool to fuel her volatile personality like this, Ethan chided himself. But that didn't stop him from prodding her further. "I won't come back to pull your pretty little behind out of the fire."

She grit her teeth. "I am perfectly capable of taking care of my own...behind, Bradshaw. In fact, I think I've been both adept and creative in doing just that—until now."

"Creative?" Ethan sputtered a harsh laugh, genuinely glad to see the old, feisty Felicia emerge again.

"You think otherwise?" she challenged.

"You, Miss High Horse, are a one-trick pony." He tapped the tip of her pert nose. "If you can't buy your way out of a situation, you're lost."

"Find what works and use it, I always say."

"Sounds more like your father's motto than your own." Ethan narrowed his eyes to observe Felicia's less-than-subtle reaction to his verbal jab. Pink, the color of the Texas sky at sunset, washed her cheeks. Her lush lips pursed, but did not open. She thrust her chest out and he savored the sight of her round breasts rising and falling in heavy rhythm.

A rush of exuberance and lust roared through his veins. His lips twitched, then stretched into a triumphant grin. "Besides, Felicia," he said, pushing her just one step further than was prudent, "your methodology seems to have stopped working about one cowboy and five hundred dollars ago."

"Why, I ought to..."

"Don't bother finishing that sentence, sweetheart." He gripped the door and leaned down to place his face directly over hers. "Because if it's one thing I've learned about you—you *never* do what you *ought* to do."

"That shows just how little you do know about me, then, Bradshaw," she said, bitterness infusing her voice. "Because up until last night, my whole life centered on what I *ought* to do and be—having nothing to do with my own wants, needs or dreams."

She shoved her belongings behind the passenger seat and climbed inside the Blazer.

Ethan shut the door after her, then moved around to the driver's side in silence. Even if her revelation hadn't been meaty enough to be called food for thought, it certainly gave him something to chew on.

Once or twice during the next few hours, he wanted to ask her to elaborate on her remark, but he knew he would be wasting his time. Besides, given his overzealous libido where Felicia was concerned, it was probably better if he didn't let anything stir up sympathetic feelings for her. She was, after all, another man's fiancée.

"I really need to call Todd," she said as if she'd been privy to his thoughts. "I just saw a sign for a gas station ten miles ahead. If it wouldn't throw you off schedule, I'd like to stop."

Ethan nodded. "But you'll have to make it brief—and don't tell him where we are, what route we're taking or be specific about when we'll arrive."

"Are you kidding?"

"No. I'm not kidding." He threw her a perturbed glance. "Think about it, Felicia. Your father has to know you'll try to contact Loverboy."

"Yes, but it's not like Father will have Todd's phone bugged." She slouched, pressing her back to the seat. "He hasn't had nearly enough time to accomplish something like that."

"Phone tapping is illegal," Ethan reminded her. "Not even Gower Grantham would stoop to breaking the law just to spy on your fiancé."

"And you think *I'm* naive." She laughed. "Anyway, the point is, I think it's safe to tell Todd about our plans."

"And I say no." He slashed his hand through the air. "The less Armstrong knows, the less he can let slip."

She batted her thick lashes at him. "Then that will be a brief phone call."

Ethan squirmed and squinted at the long strip of road rolling out toward infinity before them. "Long enough for the two of you to get all the mushy stuff out of the way, I reckon."

"Yeah, right." Felicia rolled her eyes.

Again, Ethan fought back the temptation to try to wheedle more information out of her. But he couldn't dismiss the definite pattern he saw in her benign references to Todd Armstrong. This was not your typical whirlwind love match. If he doubted that, the curt way in which Felicia dealt with Armstrong over the phone a few minutes later confirmed it for him.

He focused his camera lens on her profile. Even with the black pay phone covering half her face, he could see the traces of anxiety in her features. He contemplated not taking the picture, chided himself for acting soft, then snapped the photo. At the sound, Felicia lifted her head to glare at him.

"A deal's a deal," he said, pointing the lens at her again.

She paused, twisted the mouthpiece away from her lips, and shook her head. Spirals of ink-black hair spilled over her shoulders and framed her perfect breasts, made even more tantalizing by the snug pink shirt she wore.

Ethan gulped down the lump in his throat. If only it were that easy to suppress the desire that had arisen in his lower regions. He forced his mind back to his job and zeroed his lens on Felicia again.

She sighed in resignation. Her beautiful black eyes fixed on the ceiling.

"Is that the way you want to be seen in national magazines?" Ethan warned. The pads of his fingers flattened against the textured sides of his camera. "I'll give you two seconds to put on a pretty face."

"Okay, how's this?" She dropped her chin, crossed her eyes and stuck her tongue out right at him.

Ethan bit his cheek to keep any response at bay and got the picture. Felicia laughed and broke into the brightest, most natural smile he'd seen since they'd joined forces. He snapped another shot—for himself.

Moments later, Felicia hung up the phone. She met him at the gas station counter just as the attendant finished counting out his change. Ethan quickly stuffed the jangling coins in his pocket and faced Felicia. "You look worried. What is it?"

"Todd says..." She glanced over at the attendant.

Ethan stepped over and took her arm. He shepherded her down a vacant aisle, keeping her tucked close so they could speak in whispers.

"Is there a problem?" he asked.

Felicia raised her enormous eyes. "Todd says the press is all over him."

"And I'll bet he's loving every minute of it."

"That's beside the point," she snapped.

"Aw, c'mon, Felicia, what's the matter? From what I've read in the past, you've never been hampered by a few tabloid paparazzi snooping around."

"If only that's all it was, Bradshaw." She clutched at his arm. "But the legitimate press is in on this now."

"No way." Her touch mesmerized him. He thrust his hands in his pockets to prevent himself from taking her in his arms. "Why would anyone but a few tabloid freelancers be interested in this?"

She curled her fingers into his tight bicep. "Because," she whispered fiercely, "it has all the things that pique the public's interest—money, mystery, romance."

"Did you say mystery?"

"Of course, mystery. As far as my father knows, I disappeared into thin air last night."

The chaotic sounds of the station crescendoed in Ethan's ears. His stomach lurched. His mind raced toward a thousand different solutions to their present predicament. Before he could reach one, a tall man rounded the corner and headed down the aisle toward them.

On instinct, Ethan wrapped Felicia in a close embrace.

"Hey," she croaked in a hoarse voice. She crammed her arms between their bodies, her elbows poking at Ethan's ribs.

"Calm down," Ethan murmured in her ear. For the ears of the approaching man, he said loudly, "Now, none of that, darling. We're in a public place."

The man grimaced in their direction. Ethan chuckled a bit too robustly and told the stranger, "Still on our honeymoon."

"Congratulations," the man muttered, hurrying past.

When he had disappeared, Ethan released Felicia, who in turn, released her wrath on his chest.

"What was that for?" Ethan rubbed the spot where her palm had landed.

"For mauling me for no good reason."

"I had a reason," Ethan protested. "You just told me that the press is on to you and that your dad thinks you've disappeared. That man could have been anyone from a tabloid journalist to a detective. I had to hide your identity."

"So you thought you'd use that old chestnut of laying a big old kiss on me to obscure my face?"

Her face glowed a becoming shade of rose. Her mouth remained parted. Ethan blinked down at the sight. He cocked his head and let his gaze settle into hers. Seconds passed. The odor of gas and food from the station faded and the warm scent of the woman permeated his senses. He slicked the tip of his tongue over his dry lips. "Pardon me for pointing out the obvious, princess. But I did not kiss you."

"But you meant to," she accused.

"No." He touched her nose with one fingertip. "If I had meant to kiss you, you'd still be recovering from the act."

He turned on his heel and started down the aisle.

"So you say," Felicia scoffed. She planted her feet to keep her wobbling knees from giving away her true reaction to Ethan's claim.

"So I *know.*" He didn't even look back.

"Not like you'll ever find out." She crossed her arms and drew in a faltering breath.

"Guess not." He sauntered to the end of the row of packaged food, then halted. "Unless..."

Fast and powerful, like heat lightning, Ethan spun on his heel, strode back to her and pulled her to him.

Felicia only had time to moan in surprised delight before his mouth fit over hers.

The kiss was all clash and clarity. Hot skin, cold sweat. The softness of her feminine form yearning to meld with the hardness of Ethan's masculinity. After fifteen years of waiting and wondering, she was finally in Ethan Bradshaw's arms. Without a doubt, she knew now that no man would ever make her feel the way that he did.

She dug her fingers into the crisp cotton of his shirt. He feasted on her lips like a starving man. She savored every nuance as if she, too, had to get her fill. When he pulled away, a tiny whimper followed him from her tingling lips.

"Now we both know," he whispered.

The distant, smoky look in his eyes and the deep flush on his angular face spoke volumes. Nothing else remained to be said. Felicia nodded and stepped away from him.

He excused himself, telling her he wanted to check in with his old boss at the news bureau to see what he could uncover about her story.

Felicia bought a soft drink and a candy bar, all the time keeping her eyes on the man who had just redefined desire for her. He towered over the dirty pay phone even without wearing his big Stetson. Still, there was a gracefulness about his movements that showed he was not the typical stiff-jointed cowpoke that he appeared to be. As he conversed with the unseen party, he gestured and paced—as much as the short silver cord would allow.

Grudging admiration and sincere gratitude welled up within her. As a child, she'd seen him as a someone to escape and outwit. In her young teens, she'd thought him her mentor and confidant. At sixteen, she'd convinced herself that the sun didn't rise until he opened his eyes. He was her everything—until he'd crushed her with one ruthless act. Since then, she'd pushed any thoughts of him aside. He had become the enemy.

She studied him now, making arrangements to help her achieve her goal. Whatever else Ethan Bradshaw was, for this tiny moment in time, he was her hero. Despite her lack of practice choosing champions, she'd certainly found one in him, a man she could trust, confide in and—if she let herself—love. She sighed and swept the back of her hand over her lips.

Ethan appeared to bark a few more words into the mouthpiece, then slammed the receiver down. In three long strides, he was at her side.

"What did you find out?" she asked, hoping she didn't sound too breathless and adoring.

"Well, for starters, your fiancé was right. You've caused an all-out media blitz."

"Uh-oh."

"And on top of that, your father has offered a sizable reward to anyone who gives a tip that leads the police to you."

"So?" She shrugged. "The only one who could tip off the police is you."

"And that Drake fellow you paid to take you to Las Vegas," Ethan grumbled.

"Oh, my." Her heart plummeted. She tried to swallow but her throat disobeyed the command. Instead, she gulped in a mouthful of air. Her hand shot out and snatched Ethan's sleeve. "What do we do now?"

Ethan's gaze honed in on hers. His eyes flashed like cold steel. "I've already exercised the only option open to us."

Felicia's blood chilled. Her neck and wrists went clammy at the pulse points. Still, one thought kept her from forsaking all hope. "Whatever you did, Ethan, I know it was the right thing. If there's one thing I've learned in the last twelve hours, it's that I can trust you to put my best interest first."

He huffed out a hard burst of air, set his jaw and narrowed his eyes at her, clearly uncomfortable with her praise.

Felicia gripped her hand on his arm. "Okay, so what positively brilliant move have you made on my behalf?"

He winced, cleared his throat, then met her gaze squarely, almost daring her to respond as he said, "I told my bureau chief exactly where we are and exactly what we're up to."

Chapter Four

"You have got to be kidding," Felicia said several hours later as she gripped her hands on the stiff denim over her hips. "Tell me you're kidding, Bradshaw."

Ethan fixed a sober expression on her. With cool detachment, he raised one eyebrow to show his opinion of her outburst. "No, I'm not kidding. And neither is the bureau chief. If you want to get back to Las Vegas without your father or the media swooping down on you, this is the only way to go."

Felicia gulped down the blistering reply she longed to give, aware that she and Ethan were not alone. She glanced at the pair of reporters sent out by Ethan's ex-boss and strained a smile. Then she let her attention fall fully on the means of transportation they had delivered for her salvation. A heavy sigh scalded her lungs as she released her unspoken agitation.

"It's not so bad, Ms. Grantham," the lanky young male reporter said.

"Not so bad?" Felicia feigned a sharp choking sound deep in her throat. "It's a . . ." She waved her upturned hands at the nondescript rental car and the boxed wagon contraption attached to it. "Well, I don't even *know* what it is."

"It's a camper," Ethan muttered, his impatience beginning to crease lines around his taut lips. He adjusted his opaque black hat until a blue-gray shadow slashed across his eyes and nose. "You do know what a camper is, don't you?"

"Yes." The word seeped through her clenched teeth with a drawn-out hiss. "I know what a camper is, but I still don't know what this thing is. It's certainly not big enough for one person to sleep in, much less two."

She glanced around the nearly deserted rest stop on the stretch of old Texas interstate, then approached the strange container with caution. A thin strip of chrome trim winked in the bright afternoon sun. Felicia leaned over the waist-high object and shook her head. "When you said you'd taken care of everything, I pictured a helicopter, a limo or, at the very least, an RV. But this?"

"This will get the job done." Ethan moved beside her. "In exchange for help getting to Las Vegas, Bob Harding, my ex-boss, wanted the exclusive rights to the chronicle of your trip. It would hardly be worth their time and effort for a few snapshots of you boarding a helicopter, now would it?"

"What about a limo?"

"A limo? Why don't we just paint a big red sign on our backs?" He swept his hands in front of his face as if reading a proclamation. "Felicia Grantham in here." He garbled a curse and kicked at the red dirt under his foot. "The countryside will be crawling with press. What would stick out more than a long white limo cruising the highway from Texas to Nevada?''

"An RV, then. That wouldn't look too suspicious.'' She met Ethan's glare with equal veracity, tossing her hair in cocky one-upmanship. The moment the thick mane lifted from her hot neck, a cool breeze skimmed over the exposed damp skin. She shuddered but she did not blink. She just kept her eyes level with Ethan's. "At least with an RV I'd be able to escape a certain male presence by riding in the back.''

"You want to ride in the back?'' Ethan jerked his thumb over his shoulder.

Felicia braced herself.

"Then you can just ride in the back.'' Ethan opened his hand and brought it down with a resounding bang on the top of the compact camper.

The two reporters standing nearby jumped and gasped.

"Just let me pop this little baby up and you can climb right in,'' Ethan continued. His eyes narrowed to slits beneath the brim of his hat. "Mind you, when I fold the camper back down you're likely to get all bent out of shape. But, then, that seems to be your natural state, doesn't it?''

Felicia crossed her arms under her breasts. And to think, a few hours ago she'd been ready to trust this man implicitly. Now...

She drew in a dry, dusty breath. Now she was seeing things through more realistic eyes. Though she still had every reason to trust Ethan, she had to keep in mind that his main goal on this journey was not to aid and abet her flight. Revenging the wrongs her father had done his family motivated Ethan Bradshaw. No matter how great a kisser he was, Felicia could never let herself get all sappy over him again.

"The only thing that's bent around here is your sense of humor, Bradshaw," she said with quiet control. "Now, as for that crack about my natural state..."

She gave a purposeful pause, shifting her weight so that her hips moved just enough to draw Ethan's attention. Sweat beaded on his upper lip.

"What about your—" Ethan's Adam's apple sank and rose again in a slow, tense swallow "—natural state?"

She whirled around and walked away. Just as she popped open the car door, she nailed him with a sultry smirk. "It's not really any of your concern, is it? After all, you only have to endure it for a couple days."

"Those'll be two of the longest days of my life, I'm sure," he muttered, tearing his hat from his head and tossing it inside his parked Blazer.

"I don't doubt that," the fresh voice of the woman reporter interjected. "Just spending twenty minutes with you two has aged me considerably. Are you sure you'll both survive this little sojourn?"

"They'll be fine," the man at her side said. "But the longer we hang around, the greater the chance they have of getting caught."

He thrust out his hand. Ethan struggled for a moment to extract his keys from the pocket of his snug-fitting jeans. Felicia lowered her lashes to cover her naked admiration of Ethan's physique. If she let herself, she could easily imagine him in his own "natural state." She tried to put the rogue impulse out of her head, but that was a little like not trying to think of elephants when somebody says, "Don't think of elephants."

She ran one hand down her neck to brush away a stray rivulet of sweat. Without her consent, her eyes fluttered shut and an unbridled vision of Ethan's body, bare in back view filled her mind. Sun glistened off his broad shoulders and highlighted the tanned skin of his back. His behind, as evidenced by what she had seen in his jeans, was round with perfect hollows on each side. And since he didn't seem the type for nude sunbathing, it would be...

Suddenly, the sharp jangling of keys falling broke through her reverie. The figment of her libido fled from the sound like a skittish ghost. Her eyes flew open just in time to catch Ethan giving last-minute instructions to their helpers.

"Don't worry about how many miles you have to put on the truck. Just drive around the entire area and let yourselves be seen." He glanced over at the young woman. "But not looking like that. Did you bring a wig?"

The woman nodded.

"Why would she need a wig?" Felicia asked, hoping no one noticed the husky traces in her tone.

"Well, she wouldn't be much of a decoy for you if she drove around looking like herself, now would she?" Ethan squinted out at the barren Texas horizon as he answered.

"A decoy?" Felicia finally let herself drop into the passenger seat of the rental car, but she didn't close the door. "Is that really necessary? I mean, no one knows for certain that we're in this area. There's more than one route from Texas to Nevada, you know."

"Yes, but this route has eyewitnesses that can place you in Smokewater as of this morning," the young woman said in a voice that must have been aiming at boredom but sounded impatient.

"Eyewitnesses?" A cold sensation swelled in Felicia's belly. "Who could there be but Drake?"

"Oh, let's see." The woman sighed and began to tick off the numbers on her hand. "There's the waitress, and several men at the diner who verified that you were offering money for a ride to Las Vegas. They all identified your photo."

Ethan tipped his chin upward and swore at the sun.

"But the worst is the lady in the town store," the male reporter said, almost apologetically. "She said you tried to pay for some clothes with a credit card, leaving no doubt as to who you were."

Ethan dropped his hard gaze to her. "Tell me you didn't do that."

"I wanted to save my cash for the trip," she whined, lamely defending an action she knew had been downright foolish.

"Save your cash?" Ethan slapped his hand to his thigh. "Kind of an ironic statement from someone who handed five hundred dollars to a stranger in a diner."

"I had no choice." Felicia pulled herself up out of the car. "You left me high and dry."

Ethan marched up to her, his eyes flashing. "Well, I never would have left you if you hadn't acted so mule-headed."

"Mule-headed? Now there's irony." She jutted her chin at him, her hands clamped on her hips. "Being called mule-headed by someone with all the charm of a donkey's behind."

"You want to tell me about charm?" Ethan edged closer, his hot breath swathing her face. "Lady, I've met machine-gun-toting terrorists with more charm than you and they were a damn sight quieter, too."

"Quiet?" Felicia stretched up on tiptoe, pushing her chest up and out to meet his. Her breath caught in her throat, then blasted out with the echoed word. "Quiet? You're complaining to me about quiet? After all your blustering and bravado? I can't believe my ears."

"What a coincidence." He bent over her until she had to arch her back to keep his full face in view. "I can't believe your mouth."

"Oh, yeah?" She poked her finger into his chest. "I can't believe your—"

Felicia's sentiment was cut short by the crash of two doors slamming shut simultaneously. Both she and Ethan spun to face the sound.

"If we don't see you two in Vegas in a few days, we'll know you killed each other," the woman reporter called out the window of Ethan's Blazer.

The male reporter plunked Ethan's Stetson on his own head, then gunned the motor. He leaned forward, touching two fingers to the hat brim in a half salute. The woman arranged the disheveled strands of a black wig to partially conceal her face, then she, too, waved farewell. The tires ground against the red dirt crusted on the rest stop parking lot. The pair roared off in a cloud of rust-colored dust, leaving behind the olive-drab duffel and Ethan's suitcase which they'd taken from the Blazer earlier.

Ethan shook his head. The sweltering Texas sun sent a streak of cobalt blue zigzagging over his black hair. "What's with them?"

Felicia shrugged. "You'd think they'd never seen two people voice a difference of opinion."

Ethan cocked his head, shut his eyes, then let his lips roll up in a slow, wincing smile. A soft, tension-busting chuckle vibrated up through his chest. In moments, Felicia's lilting laughter complimented his deeper tones.

"C'mon," he said, his cheeks still stretched tight in a self-mocking grin. He motioned for her to get in the rental car, and after collecting their things, he did the same.

Felicia slid into the upholstered bucket seat and immediately fixed her attention on the mundane tasks of preparing to go.

"Let's see if we can't make up some lost ground," Ethan said softly. He stole a sidelong glimpse at her to see if she'd taken his remark as personally as he had meant it.

The sharp chink of the safety belt sliding into place answered him. Okay, so Felicia wasn't ready to forgive him for involving others in her great escape. Considering how fiercely she needed to believe that she was masterminding everything, that shouldn't surprise him.

Ethan pulled onto the almost-forsaken stretch of road and headed west. Try as he might, he could not engage Felicia in any conversation more serious than plotting their itinerary.

He settled back in his seat, letting her fuss over the cumbersome atlas. She flipped pages, highlighted possible routes, calculated mileage. All harmless diversions that made her feel better, even if he'd already made up his mind precisely how he would get them to their destination.

"If we spend the night just west of Albuquerque we'll only be one day's drive out of Vegas." Felicia snapped the lid back on her highlighter pen, then tapped it on the page above the spot where she expected them to stay.

Ethan shot his hand out to still the annoying popping of pen on paper. "I've already decided where we're going to spend the night, thank you."

"Oh, and I can just guess where that is," Felicia said, laying her pen against her cheek.

"You can?"

"Absolutely." She batted away a curl of black hair which had fallen over her eyes. "You want to stay *east* of Albuquerque. Or *north* of Albuquerque. Or *south* of—"

"I get your point."

"You'd even rather set up camp right smack-dab in the heart of downtown Albuquerque," she half shouted, "than concede to stop anywhere that I suggest. Am I right?"

"Not often, from what I can tell." He checked the rearview mirror for signs of life on the empty road. "And before you jump all over me..."

She opened her mouth.

He cut short any sassy remark with a leer and a wink.

Her eyes and lips narrowed in unison.

"Before you jump all over me..."

"You already said that."

"Yeah, but it sounded so good, I decided to say it again." He paused a moment to revel in her obvious irritation with him. "But back to the subject of where we'll spend the night. I've already selected a secluded campgrounds a few miles off the highway."

"How far off?" She crossed her arms and angled her shoulders to create a defensive wall of her upper body. "And just how much time will we lose by taking this unscheduled jaunt?"

"Jaunt?" Ethan's nose twitched just saying the silly word. "Listen, Miss High Horse, this is neither a jaunt nor is it unscheduled. I took the trouble to chart out the best course plus two alternatives while we waited for the camper."

"You did? But I..." She smacked the atlas with the back of her hand. "Why didn't you say something before now?"

"Same reason I didn't bring it to your attention when I exited the highway about twenty miles back." He nodded toward the deserted road extending into the dusk. "Telling you would only cause another argument."

"You got that right, bub." She tensed her crossed arms, unintentionally pushing her breasts up against the straining pink fabric of her T-shirt. "Still, it seems beneath even you to stoop to petty duplicity. Surely, you can do better."

You have no idea how much better I can do. He flexed his tingling thigh muscles and, much like when they were younger, made himself play the tough guy.

He barked a laugh, then let his gaze stray from the road to her face, taking an obvious detour over her well-displayed assets. "I do what suits me, Felicia, and whatever I feel is necessary to get my job done. The sooner you get that through your hard little head, the better we'll get along."

"What's that supposed to mean?" She glowered at him.

"It means that I'm not your servant. I'm not impressed by your daddy, your money or your..." His gaze dipped again to her breasts.

She readjusted her arms ever so slightly and shifted her hips. "My what?"

"Your demeanor." He stretched the word out until it sounded positively obscene. "If you haven't picked that up from what I've said today, then perhaps you should call on past experience." His lips stiffened with every word. "I am my own man. I do things for my own reasons."

"I know that, Bradshaw. I know that." She slumped in the seat, her shiny hair tangling over the drab gray upholstery. "That doesn't mean you have to ignore my input entirely. Or refuse to answer my questions."

"I'll gladly answer your questions when they're put to me as questions, not demands," he barked.

"Oh, pardon me for violating your personal code of etiquette, Bradshaw." She kicked the imitation leather dash with the toe of her sneaker. Twisting to face him, she batted her eyes. "If it's not too much trouble, Mr. Bradshaw, would you please do me the courtesy of telling me where this campground is?"

"No trouble at all, Ms. Grantham," he said, refusing to give her the satisfaction of getting annoyed by her sarcasm. "It's about forty feet in front of your precocious pug nose, if you'd care to sit properly in your seat and look for it."

Ethan swung the car and its ungangly attachment onto a gravel drive. Even in the dimming evening light, the brown-and-yellow painted sign clearly identified the small grounds as Camper's Haven.

"Haven?" Felicia scoffed. "It looks more like..."

"Like what?"

Felicia blinked at him, visibly considering whether to launch them into another squall. Mercifully, she veered clear of further conflict. "It looks fine, Bradshaw."

"Good." He cut the engine, then pushed open the car door. "Try to look inconspicuous. I'm going into the office and get us a spot."

Inconspicuous. Felicia hunched down in the seat until she could rest her temple against the padded ledge below the window. Unconscious. That's what she'd rather be. Every muscle in her body throbbed with a weariness she'd never known. The only thing she looked forward to now was finally getting a good night's sleep. The creek and bang of a screen door opening and slamming drew Felicia's attention. Ethan's shadowy figure had disappeared inside the rustic office cabin. She peered out the window, her eyes straining to make out the surroundings in the fast-approaching darkness.

"Not exactly the life to which I am accustomed," she muttered as she surveyed the place and sighed. What had she gotten herself into? She swatted away a tiny bug buzzing around her head. More importantly, when would it all be over?

She waited impatiently for Ethan to emerge from the sparsely lit cabin, holding her breath to keep from inhaling the faint odor of garbage and burning charcoal. A fine layer of dirt covered everything she saw—the signs, the trash cans, the telephone.

"The telephone." If she hadn't felt her lips move, she wouldn't have believed she'd actually voiced the thought. She blinked to make sure she hadn't dreamed the image, as well. But when she looked again, there it was. A lone pay phone, the porch light gleaming off its muted silver like a welcoming beacon.

One quarter. That was all it would take. One quarter deposited in that trusty public phone and she could end this whole miserable adventure. She bent to reach for her purse on the floorboard, her mind racing to list the pros and cons of contacting someone to come and get her.

She wouldn't have to look far to find her first reason in favor of placing that call. It was right behind her. Or right behind her car, to be precise. She'd never slept in a collapsible camper, but it couldn't be the most comfortable place in the world.

She huffed, struggling to unwind her purse's strap from a lever on the front of the seat. Number two on the list, she continued mentally, involved bathing—or lack of. She'd gladly give every penny of the ninety-two dollars she still had for an hour-long, steamy bubble bath. She could only imagine what kind of limited facilities this place had.

She poked her fingers down into the dark recesses under the car seat to try and untangle the stubborn purse strap. A curse slipped from her frowning lips. A low grumbling answered her frustration. She pressed her hand to her empty stomach. Reason number three: all she could eat at the finest restaurant she could imagine.

"Reason number four," she ground out from between her clenched teeth as she manipulated the soft leather strap coiled around the cold metal lever. Reason number four: calling would certainly ease her father's mind. She paused in her efforts.

Her father. He had to be worried sick about her. How could she let that continue? All those news stories. And the false leads, some of which she had helped create by agreeing to Ethan's decoy couple. That had to be hard on him. Guilt stabbed at her heart.

How could she have been so thoughtless? Warm tears beaded up in the corners of her eyes. As if she wasn't in enough of a frazzled emotional state. But thinking of her father scanning the veritable sea of information provided by his private piranhas made her...

She paused. It made her blood boil. By now her father had to know that she was alive. That she was acting of her own volition and had not been kidnapped. That she was determined to get on with her plans and with her life in spite of his tricks and treachery.

"Strike reason number four for calling," she whispered roughly. She clutched her purse strap firmly in her fist. Amend that. The new reason number four would be that calling might take away some of her father's power over her. If she called off the chase, then it would be on her terms. "Sort of."

She winced. Maybe she should think of reasons not to call, she decided. She gripped her purse strap until the malleable leather molded like warm clay to her palm. Her mind replayed the disastrous events of the past day. But not a single reason sprang forth to prevent her from using that waiting pay phone.

Okay, then, she thought as she tensed her arm and gave one final tug to free her purse. The strap gave. The prolonged growl of rows of stitching ripping loose filled the car.

Momentum from her exertion threw her upright just in time to see Ethan exit the shabby office. The light over his head touched his black hair and melted over it like molten gold. He lifted his face to gaze in her direction. Shadows both hid and highlighted his features, sending an inexplicable thrill through Felicia's being. Without the penetrating presence of his searching eyes, his face took on a wary sophistication that she had never noticed. An aged-by-grace quality that told of both his life of high adventure and his longing for. . .

She placed her hand at her throat and tried to swallow. She could not define what Ethan Bradshaw longed for. She wondered if he even could—and if it would surprise him that she felt that same kind of indistinct, yet overwhelming, yearning in herself.

He stopped to run his splayed fingers through his hair, then stepped from the yellow spotlight on the porch. Felicia exhaled, releasing a lazy swirl of oxygen inside her head. She must have been holding her breath longer than she realized.

Still, she hadn't lost her train of thought. She'd been composing a list of reasons for and against making a phone call.

Ethan's boots scuffed over the dirt and gravel drive, coming closer.

So far, the list in favor had four very good reasons on it.

Ethan stopped beside the car.

The list against the call had only one. Ethan.

He put out his hand and wrapped it around the door handle.

That one reason was more than enough. She shut her eyes and sank her teeth into her lower lip. Heaven help her, but she wanted to spend just a little more time with Ethan. If that meant she reached her goal and attained blessed freedom, then all the better.

Ethan pulled open the door. The car dipped slightly toward his side as he dropped into the driver's seat. "Wake up, princess," he said. "We've got a lot of work to do before we can afford the luxury of falling into bed."

Felicia's skin prickled up into a million goose bumps. She knew he hadn't meant it as an invitation, but hearing any mention of bed in Ethan Bradshaw's sexy baritone voice thrilled her in every delicious way. She sighed and forced her eyes open before she made a darned fool of herself.

"Did you say—" she swallowed "—work?"

"Yes, work," he snapped. "What did you think, that the camper would set itself up?" He started the engine and flipped on the headlights. Slowly he began to guide the car down a winding path, between small plots occupied by other campers. "We've got to put the camper up, get a lantern going, then attend to a few, um, personal things."

"Then can we get some sleep?" She pretended to be exasperated by the insignificant list of chores, to ensure he couldn't guess how much she looked forward to spending the night near him.

"Not unless you want to sleep standing up." He turned the car hard to the left. Orange-red campfires and the yellow glow of electric bulbs from inside expensive RVs lit their way as he drove on. "After we do all that, we still have to make our beds."

There was that word again. Felicia's spine tingled. Up until a few moments ago, she hadn't considered that she and Ethan would be sleeping under one, very compact roof. All she had thought about was rest.

Ethan must have interpreted her silence for sulking, because his tone sharpened as he turned toward her and asked, "You do know how to make a bed, don't you, Miss High Horse?"

"Let's see," she said, acting every bit the silly, spoiled incompetent he insisted on pretending she was. She placed a finger to her cheek and gazed off into space. "I can make reservations, make small talk, even make believe that you're a civilized traveling companion."

"All well and good." His tone told her that he was on to her game and playing along. He pulled the car into an empty spot and shut the engine off before turning to face her. Even in the dim light, his eyes glinted. His teeth flashed unnaturally white in the rising moonlight. He leaned across the seat and finished his comment in a hoarse whisper, "But I asked about a bed."

Not since he had kissed her had Felicia felt this rush of pure hormonal power. It swept over her like a gale force wind and tore the clever, confident answer out of her mind. She opened her mouth. She blinked. Ethan's eyes bore into hers. She blinked again and finally managed to stammer in a tiny voice, "Um, uh, I can make a bed."

"Good." He tipped his head to her, then got out of the car.

Felicia squeezed her eyes shut, commanding away the flush of embarrassment and lust she'd just experienced.

"Hey." Ethan poked his head back inside the car.

Felicia clutched at her heart, attempting to recover from his sudden and very loud interruption. "What?"

"What? We've got a lot to do, that's what. Now, are you with me or not?"

Felicia sighed and popped open her door. Getting out in a rolling movement, she couldn't help muttering to herself, "Yes, I'm with you, Bradshaw, no matter how hard I try to fight it. I'm with you one hundred percent."

Chapter Five

"No, no, no. You're doing it all wrong."

Ethan straightened his aching back and glared at Felicia. "Suddenly you're an expert on setting up a compact camper?"

She wrestled to lift up the kerosene lantern they'd retrieved from the trunk, then pointed to the circle of hazy light it cast. "I don't have to be an expert to know that when you turn that crank, the camper is supposed to go up—not groan then quiver like a mass of Jell-O."

Jeez. He hated it when she was right. Ethan released his death grip on the icy crank handle. "I suppose you have a suggestion."

"Well . . ." She cocked her head. The light washed over her face. She nipped the tip of one finger between her perfect white teeth.

Even in his weary state, Ethan found the image erotic. Only the fact that he expected to be thoroughly exhausted gave him any hope that he would get any sleep sharing the camper with Felicia. The realization egged his testy temper further on. "Well, what?"

She dropped her hand from her face. "Are you sure you're turning the crank the right way?"

"Am I...?" He caught himself before he launched into a nonproductive but totally satisfying tirade. With a chivalrous bow, he extended his arm toward the unbudging camper. "Obviously, you think I'm too dense to manage this. Why don't you give it a try?"

"Okay, I will." She thrust the lantern at him.

"Be my guest." He accepted the metal handle of the camp lantern.

She nodded to him, then sized up the task with one eye closed. Her hair bounced around her shoulders when she drew them up, making a show of inhaling.

Ethan smiled at the display.

She bent down to closer examine the crooked crank jutting out from the side of the half-mast camper.

Ethan leaned back, trying to throw her by openly regarding her backside. Unfortunately, the ploy had a greater effect on him than it did on her.

She simply glanced back at him and clicked her tongue.

He swallowed hard and shifted his weight.

"I think I see what to do," Felicia said.

"Want me to give it a go?"

"No." She motioned for him to stand aside. When he did, she held her hands up and spit lightly into the palms, like a burly lumberjack.

A burst of silent laughter caught in Ethan's throat. Regardless of what he thought of her upbringing, she was game for just about anything. He had to admire that.

She curled both hands around the crank and gave it a big heave. Metal ground against metal, tearing through the quiet night. Felicia gave it another mighty shove. The camper squawked again in complaint of her rough treatment. It shuddered. Then, with all the grace of a hippo lumbering out of a mud hole, it began to move upward.

"Well, I'll be damned," Ethan muttered.

"Hey, stop lamenting your fate and get busy. This campsite isn't going to spring to life by itself, you know," Felicia called out in triumph and joy.

The rest of the work went easily and with Ethan and Felicia's unflagging effort, was done in no time.

"I have to admit, Felicia, you really put your back into it," Ethan said as he climbed into the camper behind her.

"Well, what did you expect?" she asked over the clack of setting the lantern on the tiny table.

Ethan gave a defensive shrug. "I don't know.... That you'd at least whine about ruining your manicure."

"Sorry to disappoint you—" she spun and fixed her gaze on his "—again."

Nothing he could say to that, he guessed. He glanced away just long enough to let her know he'd received her admonishment. When he returned his gaze to hers, he said, "I know I've been unusually hard on you, Felicia. But this is not the kind of thing I'm used to doing. And you're not the kind of woman I'm used to dealing with."

"Oh?" She clasped her hands in front of her, her expression earnest. "What kind of woman do you usually deal with, Bradshaw?"

"Forget I said that," he muttered, dropping to the thin cushion on the bench seat on the opposite side of the table from where Felicia stood.

"No," she said, crossing her arms. She brought one knee up to rest on the bench paralleling Ethan's. "I'm intrigued. How am I so different? Am I more demanding?"

He lifted his head. The golden glow of the lantern between them reflected in her dark eyes, blotting out any emotions that might have shown there. What good would it do to reveal his feelings to her? He reached out and turned the key on the lantern, lowering its light to a soft glow. Everything beyond the table faded to darkness and he sighed. "This is a totally frivolous conversation, Felicia. It's late and I'm bushed. Can we just get some sleep?"

She started to argue. Paused. Sighed, then shook her head. Standing on both feet again, she relented. "Okay, Bradshaw. Whatever you say. How do you want to handle the sleeping arrangements?"

Despite himself, Ethan felt a lecherous curve creep into his smile. "You sure you want my suggestion on that?"

"Actually—" she hugged her arms tightly around her rib cage and stepped back as far as the cramped quarters would allow "—I have my own idea."

The tension in Ethan's gut eased at her retreat. It was one thing to talk about mundane things in close proximity to Felicia, but when they started discussing bed...

Well, he wanted her as far away as possible—for all the good it did him. Just hearing her voice in the dimmed light enlivened his libido as much as holding any other woman in his arms would. He cleared his throat. "What's your idea?"

"Have you ever seen the old movie *It Happened One Night?*"

"I'm not sure."

"Oh, you know the one." She waved one hand in his direction. "Clark Gable and Claudette Colbert had to share a motel room and they hung a blanket up between them so they could have privacy to change."

"You plan to change? Into what? Your belly-dancer costume?"

"Well, in the movie, see..." Both hands flew as she rushed through her explanation. "Clark loaned Claudette his pajamas and..."

"I don't wear pajamas," he deadpanned.

Her gesturing hands came to rest on her hips. "I suppose you're the macho type who sleeps—" she puffed up her chest and lowered her voice "—in the raw."

Ethan laughed. "Not exactly. I'm a little too..." He leaned into the lamp's illumination and lifted one eyebrow to drive home the meaning of his double entendre. "Sensitive for that. Those sheets chafe."

A guilty giggle gurgled in Felicia's throat.

"I sleep in briefs," he continued. "Want to borrow a pair of those?"

"No, thanks."

Ethan chuckled again. "You're the only person I know that I can hear rolling their eyes. Sorry that I don't have any pajamas for you."

"I'll just sleep in my T-shirt, if it's all the same to you," she snapped.

"I hate for you to do that. It's the only thing you have to wear tomorrow." He heard her long intake of breath but cut her off before she started talking. "Unless we stop and buy you something new to wear."

"Hmm."

"Which we're not." He tapped one finger on the laminated table. "Instead, why don't I just loan you a shirt? I brought along a change of clothes from my trailer. You can have the clean shirt."

"Then you'll have to wear the same thing you wore today," she said softly. "Why don't you let me borrow the shirt you're wearing now? That way we'd both have something fresh to put on in the morning."

"Okay by me, but..."

"Then it's settled. Take it off." She unfurled her hand toward him.

Ethan stared into her empty palm. "Jeez, you really are a bossy one, demanding the shirt right off a guy's back."

"And the blanket off his bed, if you don't mind," she added.

Ethan finished unbuttoning his shirt, then let it hang open as he twisted on the bench to indicate the sleeping platform behind him. "Unfortunately, I don't have that to give you. The camper came stocked with two sleeping bags and two pillows. No extra blankets."

"What will we do for privacy?" She swayed back just enough to place her face in total darkness.

"We shut off the lantern," he said, as he did just that. He slid the soft cotton shirt from his tired shoulders, then held it out to her. "It's too dark to see anything specific and I'm too old to get excited over a silhouette against the mosquito netting. You're safe with me, princess."

She dragged the offered shirt across his palm. He sensed reluctance in the cautious movement. "But if you're still worried about your privacy, just crawl into your sleeping bag and change inside there."

"Thanks, Ethan," she whispered as she whisked the shirt away completely.

"Don't mention it. Especially not tonight. I don't want to hear another thing until morning."

Felicia clutched Ethan's shirt to her chest. She could still feel his body heat penetrating the bundled fabric, still smell his after-shave sheathing the underside of his stiff collar.

"Good night, Ethan," she murmured as she climbed up onto the platform where her sleeping bag lay. Despite the fact that she had absolutely no practice at doing it, she managed to slide into the quilted covers and out of her clothes in short order. She had just finished jamming her arms inside the sleeves of Ethan's shirt when his booming voice startled her.

"Would you quit thrashing around over there?"

She clutched the edges of the open shirt together over her naked chest. Logically, she knew he couldn't see a thing, but hearing him so close made her feel exposed in every way. Quickly she began to poke the tiny sleek buttons through their corresponding buttonholes, fighting the constricting bag as she did. Each movement caused the taffeta shell of her sleeping bag to rustle. In the otherwise silent night, it sounded like someone repeatedly wadding up a potato chip bag—with the chips still in it.

Felicia winced and pushed the last button in place. She straightened her body, then exhaled in a whoosh. "Sorry about the noise."

"Never mind. You're done now," Ethan grumbled.

Felicia's face tightened as she scrunched her eyes closed and made one last adjustment. The sleeping bag swished and crumpled around her body.

"You are done, aren't you?"

Just as surely as someone with their hands in something gooey has to scratch their nose, Felicia had to make one last move. She tensed. She told herself she could sleep on the impossibly flat pillow. She dropped her head back. It sank through the clumps of synthetic filling and promptly bumped the plywood deck beneath her. She grit her teeth. Quick and neat as possible, she sat bolt up, twisted and punched the pillow into a fluffy ball, then fell back with a sigh. "Done."

"Finally." She heard Ethan move in his own noisy bag. "Now go to sleep."

"Okay," she whispered. "I'm halfway there already."

It was a lie. Lying alone in the dark with Ethan was not conducive to sleep. The fact that she had his shirt wrapped around her like a loving embrace didn't help matters, either.

She felt the nubby fabric that had been on his skin moments ago brush her naked belly and breasts.

Be calm, she told herself. Relax. Don't think about him. Lying there. Only a few feet away. Asleep. His face serene. His jet-black hair all tousled on his stark white pillow. His sexy chest rising and falling with each long, slow breath. She inhaled and found her lungs filled with the scent clinging to Ethan's shirt. A soft moan slipped from her half-open mouth.

"Hmm?"

She bit her lip and waited to see if Ethan had more to offer than a groggy hum. Silence answered her. Disappointed, she tried again to put the man out of her head. Just don't think of him, she chided. And, for heaven's sake, she told herself sternly, don't picture him. All sprawled out. Over there. So close you can hear the hushed buzz of his slight snoring. As if he were right here, his body curled alongside her own. With her in just a shirt. And him in just his briefs.

"That's it." She sat up. "This is ridiculous."

"Wh-what?"

"I can't sleep, Ethan," she said softly. "I think maybe a short walk would help clear my mind...."

"Clear your mind?" His sleeping bag crinkled. "Of what?"

She wadded a handful of the thick flannel lining in her palm. "Oh, you know, things."

The camper jiggled. By his silhouette, Felicia could see that he lay facing her, propped up on his elbow.

"Would talking help?" he asked.

Felicia thought of the unbidden lusty images of Ethan and smiled. "Talk wasn't what I had in mind. But since you're awake. And I'm awake."

"Yes?"

His response was a deep, primitive growl in the dark that sent a shiver down Felicia's spine. Be careful what you lust for, she reminded herself, you might get it. And get it big-time.

She pulled her knees up to her chest and hugged them tightly. "Maybe we could talk until I'm sleepy."

"Great idea. Why didn't I think of that?"

"You don't have to say it like that."

"Like what?" His volume inched up a notch.

"Through your teeth," she whispered, thinking he would get the hint.

"Pardon me, princess," he said, over enunciating each syllable. "But some of us peasants haven't had fancy diction lessons."

"That is a stupid remark, even for you, Bradshaw."

"I'm tired. If you'd care to wait until morning when I'm rested, I'll come up with a real zinger."

Felicia dropped her head back to stare into the blankness above her. "You are the most exasperating man I've ever met."

"Exasperating?" he yelped. "Me?"

"Shh." Even though he couldn't possibly see it, she placed one finger to her lips. "People around us may be trying to sleep, you know."

"Oh?" he rasped. "How inconsiderate of me to keep someone awake."

"Obviously you don't feel like talking. So why don't you just go back to sleep?"

"Do what?" he screeched.

"Shh!"

"Fine then." He threw himself down and turned over. The camper jostled under the abrupt movement.

Felicia stretched her legs out in front of her.

"Go back to sleep, she says." For a man muttering, with his back turned, his words came through strong and plain—as he obviously intended. "Never, in my life, have I had to deal with a woman like that."

She slapped the taffeta bag covering. "Aha."

"What ha?"

"You said that before. That you'd never dealt with a woman like me."

"You're dreaming," he mumbled.

"I'm wide-awake and waiting for an explanation, Bradshaw."

"What's to explain? You're unique, Miss High Horse. You should feel honored."

"Then why do I feel..." She tugged the heavy sleeping bag in place under her chin. Tears burned her eyes. This was not the first time in their relationship that Ethan had dismissed her as being too much trouble. "What's so wrong with me? Am I really so awful?"

"Hey." The camper shimmied as he rolled to face her, then half sat up. "I never said that you were awful, just..."

"A pain?" She held back a sniffle.

"Well..." The outline against the tent screen showed him cocking his head.

"Surely you've dealt with a woman or two you regarded as a pain before, Ethan," she said softly. "Why is it so different with me?"

"I don't want to go into this, Felicia."

"It's my take-charge attitude, isn't it?"

"Hardly," he barked. "In my line of work all the women I meet have a take-charge attitude."

"Then it's my social status, right?" The urge to cry subsided and she sighed away the constriction in her chest. "You've never dealt with a woman who has so much money and notoriety."

A quiet chuckle wafted across on the gentle breeze. "Felicia, I've interviewed European royalty."

"Oh." She drew in her breath. Suddenly, the clean night air seemed overwhelming. Disappointment knotted in her throat. "Then it's me. Plain and simple."

"There ain't nothing plain or simple about you, Felicia."

She should have laughed. He'd meant it as a joke, no doubt. But when Felicia tried, the only sound she could make was a pathetic little mew.

Ethan muttered a curse. When he spoke, his pure frustration colored his response. "Don't get upset. I didn't mean it like that. I'm just dancing around an embarrassing truth."

She bit her lip. Her heart lightened a fraction. "What truth?"

He rolled onto his back. As Felicia waited for him to continue, she imagined his dazzling eyes boring holes in the canvas covering overhead.

"The truth," he began slowly, "is that I've never dealt with a woman who intrigued me so much. Or one that circumstances demanded I stay so completely away from."

"Including those European royals?" she teased.

"I'm not expressing myself well." In shadowed profile she watched him cover his face with his hands. His cupped palms distorted the one syllable expression he used to describe his predicament. He pushed his fingers back through his hair, then rested his head on one arm while he lay the other across his belly.

"Okay," he said finally. "Here's the deal."

"I'm listening." Intently, she added to herself.

"I've never met a woman who, through her life-style—in fact, her very birthright—represented such a total opposite of everything I believe in and cherish."

"Oh, Ethan," she managed to croak out through the incredible pressure in her chest. This was worse than when she was sixteen and he'd laughed at her youthful seduction attempt.

"Wait, I haven't finished."

She grit her teeth and made herself hold it together. "Go on."

"As I was saying, I never met anyone who seemed so wrong for me in every way and yet compelled me so completely." He drew a loud, ragged breath. "You drive me crazy, princess—mentally, emotionally and physically." He coughed and shifted his weight. "Especially physically."

"Oh, Ethan," she murmured.

"But it's wrong." His hand sliced through the air to underscore his adamant statement. "You're on your way to the marriage altar. And regardless of my disdain for your choice in husbands, I can't try to sabotage your plans for my own jollies."

Every fiber in Felicia's being wanted to shout in disagreement, yet she pushed her knuckles against her lips to prevent any outburst. Ethan spoke the truth. She had her plans and she mustn't let herself be sidetracked—especially not for "jollies." If Ethan had more to offer...

No, she wouldn't let herself think like that. Nothing short of marriage would serve her needs. A wild mindless fling with a man who held her family in contempt would only solidify her father's opinion of her as a flighty airhead requiring his unrelenting guardianship.

A chill crept over her that not even curling up in the toasty sleeping bag could quell. She shut her eyes and dampness filled the creases above and below her lashes. Willing herself not to give into the tears, she blew out a breath and firmly said, "You're right, Ethan. You're right. It's for the best."

"I'm sorry if I made you uncomfortable, Felicia." An undeniable tenderness infused his voice. "I won't mention it again."

She nodded, rustling her sleeping bag. She had no idea if he understood her message but it would have to do.

"I mean," he went on, still quietly, "because you don't share those particular... um... leanings."

She moved her head again, this time in neither a nod nor a shake.

"You don't? Do you?"

How easy it would be to confess all under the protection of the darkness.

"Felicia?"

She let her lips fall open, wanting to speak but not trusting herself.

"Felicia? Are you still awake?"

She clamped her mouth shut and commanded her body to lie motionless. Let him believe you're asleep, she told herself. In the long run, it will save you both a lot of grief. Much as she wanted to explore her interest in Ethan, common sense made her conclude as Ethan had: it was the wrong thing to do.

"Well, good night then, princess," he whispered. "Sweet dreams."

Sweet dreams? She very much doubted it. But she could rest easier knowing she'd made the right decision concerning the man across the camper from her. She set her course when she plotted her marriage of necessity to Todd

Armstrong. If she veered away from that course now—even if only for a little while—she would lose all she hoped to gain. She would never be free of her father's grasp—at least not psychologically. She would, in that one act of giving in to her nonsensical passion for Ethan Bradshaw, forever define herself as a fickle, silly girl. She wanted more than that. She wanted to be her own woman. Just like Ethan was his own man.

That thought set off an explosion of excitement in Felicia's head. Ethan simply could not be her lover. Period. But that didn't mean he couldn't be her mentor. She fisted her hands at her sides to keep herself from thrashing about with jubilance. At that exact moment she made a vow. For as long a time as she spent with Ethan, she would learn everything she could from him. She would observe him, ask questions, study him until she knew how and why he did what he did.

Snuggling down into her sleeping bag, she smiled contently to herself. Not only had she remained true to her original plan, but she had spawned a new one—one she would put in place with a vengeance beginning first thing in the morning.

Chapter Six

"Are you sure the camper will be safe here?" Felicia tugged her hairbrush through the ebony tangles spilling over her shoulder.

"Does it matter?" Ethan circled his fists over his swollen eyelids and rubbed. He had never been a morning person, but the serious lack of sleep he'd experienced over the past few days had increased the problem tenfold. "Neither of our names is on the rental agreement."

She stepped so close, he could smell the soap on her freshly scrubbed face. "But still, shouldn't we—"

"Look—" he shuffled sideways to keep some space between them "—we haven't eaten since late yesterday afternoon." He patted his stomach. "Aren't you hungry?"

She pressed her open hand to her own flat stomach and nodded. "Famished."

"Well, when we checked in, the owner of the campground gave me directions to a place he promised had the best breakfasts in the state of New Mexico." He grinned at her and wriggled his eyebrows. "How does bacon, sausage, hot coffee and a plate of pancakes swimming in maple syrup sound to you?"

"Heavenly," she breathed, her expression almost rapturous. "I can practically smell the whole meal."

Ethan struggled not to shut his eyes and inhale with her the imagined feast. His nose twitched. His stomach grumbled. Content that hunger would have subdued her need to fight him on every issue, he concluded, "Now, we can take the time to fold the camper back into a neat little box, hook it back up to the car, then drag it the ten miles to this legendary eatery, or..."

She screwed her all-too-pert nose up in distaste that echoed his tone.

Ethan reined in a smug smile and strolled over to the car. He swung open the passenger door and swept his arm out in a flourish. "Or we leave the albatross here, speed over to get something to eat and be back in less time than it would take to pack it up."

"I vote for Plan B." She strode to the car and slid inside.

"Excellent." He waited for her to settle into her seat. When she seemed nice and comfy, he let the car door fall shut. The resulting thud made her jump a foot.

Good, he thought, let her feel a little antsy. All morning long she'd put him more than a little on edge. Watching him. Hanging on his every word. Once, he'd even caught her mimicking his stance behind his back. Not in a sarcastic or mocking way, but like an actor trying to get down a characteristic for a role she was about to play. He suspected last night's confession had something to do with her behavior. But since he wasn't willing to delve into that treacherous territory again, he assumed he'd never know.

He got in the car and followed the directions he'd been given.

"*This* is your legendary eatery?" Felicia walked up to stand beside him. They both peered up at the sign over the long brick building as Felicia read aloud, "Fairmont Food and Fuel? The best breakfasts in New Mexico?"

Ethan twisted his tensed shoulders into a tight shrug. "That's what the groundskeeper told me."

"He must have been getting a kickback from the proprietor of this dump."

"And maybe he was telling the truth." Ethan crossed his arms over his chest to ward off the crisp cool of the desert morning—and to show Felicia exactly what he thought of her attitude. "Is your world really so small that you believe everyone is motivated by money?"

She reared her head like a wild horse balking at a bridle. "You'd be surprised how small my father has managed to keep my world, Bradshaw. Mostly by using people whose prime motivation *was* money."

He scuffed his boots in the gravel drive. "I suppose it's my mission, then, to use this time we have left to broaden your view, Miss High Horse."

"Surely, you don't mean...?" She hooked her thumb toward the unsavory storefront a few feet away.

"Ah, but I do." He flattened his hand on her lithe back. Ignoring the sweet sensation of Felicia's warmth filling his palm, he gave a tiny shove to propel her forward.

She staggered a half step, then glanced over her shoulder. "You'll notify my next of kin in case I don't survive?"

"I'll send Toddie-boy a telegram."

"Gee, thanks." She took another step toward the door.

"No problem," Ethan assured her. "I'm sure he'll find someone to read it to him."

She halted.

Rather than endure a tirade or worse, have to listen to Felicia extol the virtues of her questionable fiancé, Ethan shot his arm out to push the café door open. "Quit stalling, princess, and let's eat. I doubt if it will be as bad as you suspect. In my world, I've observed that a rough exterior sometimes hides a treasure."

"I've noticed that a time or two myself, Bradshaw," she said, jabbing him in the ribs with her elbow. She stepped over the threshold of the restaurant.

Engulfed. No other word could define Felicia's feeling upon entering the realm of the Fairmont Food and Fuel. Sights, sounds and smells welled up around her with all the subtlety of an ocean wave at high tide. Warm, damp air flooded over her. She pressed her hand to her temple and tried to soak it all in.

Music—loud and decidedly country—underscored the flashing maneuverings of the gingham-uniformed waitresses. It shook the worn wooden floorboards beneath her feet, sending vibrations through her lower body. The clientele, mostly burly truck driver types, shoveled in their morning fare with gusto. The scratching and dinging of forks scraping over heavy ceramic plates attested to that.

And the aroma! Felicia's stomach grumbled harder every time she inhaled the heady mix of coffee, grilled food and hot syrups. She took a long, deep breath and held it. Her mouth watered. She spun on her heel to face Ethan.

"You hate it," he deadpanned.

"Just the opposite." She pinched the cool fabric over his hard bicep. "I can't wait to get seated and order."

"Well, ordering is what you do best. Lead the way."

"There are two stools at the end of the counter." She tugged his sleeve a little harder than necessary, determined to reach those seats before anyone else spotted the opening.

She slid onto the swiveling circular stool just seconds before a haggard-looking man could claim it. Over the stranger's grumbling, she spun toward Ethan and said, "This is great. I've never eaten at a real-life café counter."

"I feel like a witness to history." Ethan rolled his eyes and pulled a laminated menu from behind a napkin holder. "Too bad I couldn't capture the moment on film."

"Cheer up." The slightest shove from her toe sent Felicia twirling. She laughed and snatched at the chrome-trimmed edge of the counter to still herself. Facing Ethan, she patted his arm. "So you miss a few good photos. It's better than drawing a lot of attention and risking someone recognizing me."

"Speaking of someone recognizing you—" Ethan raised his menu "—you have an admirer."

"Where?" She strained her neck to see around the wall the menu created. When that failed, she started to swivel herself around to steal a glance behind Ethan's back.

"Don't do that." He placed his hand on her shoulder to anchor her in place. "Just trust me. There's a man down there who can't take his eyes off you."

"Can you blame him?" She made a show of primping, reveling in the realization that stony Ethan Bradshaw was talking like a jealous boyfriend.

"I guess not." He slid his hand from her shoulder, curving it around her arm then gliding it downward until he grasped her wrist.

Felicia's heart raced at his touch. She felt the flush that had warmed her cheeks drain as quickly as her flirtatious act fell away. She met his gaze and her body responded with an eager tingling. Suddenly self-conscious, she crossed her legs. The movement coaxed the stool into a half spin.

Ethan's grip on her arm allowed him to halt her in midwhirl. One gentle tug brought her around to face him again and when she did, he held her firmly in place. "No, can't blame a man at all for noticing."

"Why, Ethan, I'm blushing." She bowed her head.

"You should be." He straightened. "You're the only adult here spinning around on her stool like it was a cheap carnival ride."

Her jaw dropped.

"Now that I think of it, it's a wonder more people aren't staring."

"Very funny." She plucked the menu from his hands and began to study it as if it contained the very secrets of life.

Ethan's annoyingly broad shoulders shook with silent laughter. If she were serious about her vow to be more like the man, she'd laugh right along with him. She hunkered down low over the menu.

"Lighten up, princess," he said. "Or I'll have to reassess my opinion of you as a good sport."

"You think of me as a good sport?" She perked up, smacking the laminated menu on the counter. "Really?"

"You pitched in with the camper, hiked over to the public rest rooms without complaining and you're willing to give this place a try." He nudged her with his shoulder and gave her a wink. "In my book, that qualifies you as a good sport."

The familiarity of the gesture buoyed Felicia's spirits again. Maybe she was already more like Ethan than she realized. She threw her shoulders back and smiled. "Guess that makes us two of a kind, Bradshaw. But I notice that being good sports hasn't gotten the waitress to us any faster."

"She's busy. She'll get to us in a minute."

"Well, when she does come by, order me a Cattleman's Special with a short stack of pancakes on the side." She pushed up from her seat, careful not to let it swivel.

Ethan's eyebrows shot up as he read the description on the menu. "Steak and eggs?"

"Medium rare and over easy." She slapped him firmly on the back. "And don't forget the pancakes. I'm going to browse around the gift shop."

Felicia heard his voice rising in response but the din of the bustling restaurant mercifully drowned him out. The cluttered gift shop proved to be just as intriguing as the café proper. Knick knacks and whatnots called to her from metal racks and dusty shelves. It was, in a manner of speaking, like being in a roadside museum of bizarre and tacky Americana.

She glanced over the rude bumper stickers, the sexually suggestive T-shirts and the souvenirs with the state's name emblazoned on them. Then a stack of caps caught her eye. Laughing, she tried on a couple, finding it difficult to choose between one with a fish head jutting out over the bill and another with a long blond ponytail dangling from the back.

She paid for a few impulse purchases, marveling at the world beyond her father's grasp. Joy and excitement washed over her as she promised to sample it all with gusto, starting with her Cattleman's Special breakfast.

Breakfast. Felicia snapped her head up. She had definitely dawdled too long in the gift shop. Panic ripped through her chest at the thought that Ethan might have stranded her once again. She rushed to the doorway between the shop and the restaurant, her eyes seeking the spot where she had left Ethan almost twenty minutes earlier.

"Thank God," she whispered in one swift release of breath. Ethan had not gone. In fact, he seemed to have made a friend in her absence. She wound her way back to him through the maze of waitresses, customers and closely placed tables. Between rehearsing her excuse for lingering in the gift shop and psyching herself into a relaxed attitude, Felicia stole glances at Ethan's companion.

Not much of a dresser, she thought, eyeing the man's rumpled jacket and wrinkled slacks. She wondered that a man who would wear such a high-quality suit would go out looking like he'd slept in it. Maybe he was a panhandler who just happened on some expensive castoffs, she concluded.

Just then, the man puffed up his chest. His face reddened. And though Felicia couldn't hear his words, she could see his mouth contort with anger. Her heart thudded in her ears. Ethan got to his feet, glowering down at the other man. The stranger poked Ethan's chest with one accusing finger, which Ethan quickly batted away. Ethan shook his head.

Felicia was close enough to hear them now. She froze in her tracks and listened.

"Look, if I was hooked up with an heiress, would I be eating in this joint?" Ethan asked.

"You might, if you were trying to slip her by the people searching for her," the stranger replied.

"Yeah, well, I don't know anything about that." Ethan shook his head again and dropped back to his seat at the counter. "I'm just an honest trucker trying to earn an honest buck. I don't know anything about a runaway rich gal. So, why don't you leave me to eat my breakfast in peace?"

Felicia swallowed hard and considered running into the bathroom to hide from whomever was looking for her. Hopefully, Ethan's pretense would be enough to throw the man off her trail and he would leave.

"Two waitresses said you came in with a young lady," the stranger insisted loudly.

Ethan nearly choked on a mouthful of hash browns. "Lady? Buddy, that was no lady, that was my wife." He wiped a napkin across his mouth and guffawed like a clod. "I've always wanted to say that."

Ethan hunched over his plate and speared a glistening sausage. Felicia could see suspicions in the stranger's eyes even as he moved away. The man took a seat that gave him the perfect vantage point for observing Ethan without further confrontation. Clearly, Ethan's act alone would not convince the man that he had the wrong couple. This problem would not disappear unless someone made it disappear. She had no doubt who that someone must be.

"Sorry to take so long, honeypie."

Ethan almost choked at the sight of Felicia slipping onto the stool next to his. At least, he thought it was Felicia. He closed one eye and made a quick survey of the woman. She wore a bright blue ball cap pushed down past her eyebrows, hiding part of her face and all of her black hair. Wire-rimmed sunglasses perched on the bridge of her nose. She winked from above one smoky gilded oval.

"Got me a new shirt in the gift shop," she said in a loud, gruff voice.

"Among other things," he whispered with a smile.

She pointed to the oversize T-shirt enveloping her small body. "Like it?"

"When God Made Man She Was Only Joking," Ethan read. He glanced over to their curious observer to make sure his response would be heard. "Why'd you want to spend your money on a dumb thing like that for?"

Felicia flicked away the phony blond ponytail attached to the back of her cap. "I bought it 'cause wearin' it makes me feel like a new woman."

Ethan fought not to burst out laughing at her altered appearance, her hokey accent and her thinly veiled joke. "Too bad *looking* at you wearing it don't *make* you a new woman—then we'd both be happy."

"Oh, just pipe down and let me eat." She hunched over her meal. "You don't want me to get heartburn, do you?"

"Baby, ever since you first laid eyes on me, your heart's been on fire." He reached over to tug at her fake hairpiece, then thought better of it. Instead, he patted her on the back. "But you ain't got time for indigestion or breakfast now. We have to get going."

"Just give me a minute." She poked a triangle of pancakes dripping with syrup into her mouth.

"We don't have a minute." He darted his eyes to indicate the man who sat watching their every move, knowing that if the fellow decided to come over, he'd see through Felicia's disguise in an instant. He motioned to the harried waitress behind the counter. "Ma'am? Can we get her meal put in a carry-out container?"

Felicia spun her stool in Ethan's direction. Defiance flashing in her eyes, she popped a piece of steak in her mouth, chewed, then washed it down with a gulp of coffee. "Surely we have time for me to eat my breakfast before we have to leave."

Ethan's shoulders stiffened as he tried to telegraph an urgent reminder with his eyes. *You're sounding and acting a little too much like the real Felicia. Cool it.* To underscore his message, he scowled at her. "Don't tell me how much time we have, woman. You let the waitress get them steak and eggs ready to go. We got to be hitting the highway."

Felicia jabbed her fork into another bite-size piece of meat, playing along again but in her own indominable style. "You let me finish up here or the only thing hitting the highway will be your flat feet after I take off in the rig without you."

"I'm shaking in my boots, girl," he bellowed.

"Don't think I won't do it," she said, her cheeks bulging with food. "I'm my own woman, damn it, and I do as I please."

Ethan suppressed his pride at hearing her use his own words about himself to describe herself to a T. Instead he mumbled something into his nearly empty coffee cup.

"What was that?"

He tossed back the bitter dregs from the cup, winced, then glared at her. "I said, and to think some yahoo thought you were an heiress."

"I hope you gave him what for." She let her fork fall onto her plate.

Above the clatter, he asked, "Why?"

"Look, honeypie, you may be hard to look at and about as sharp as a basketball but when someone calls you a name, I stick up for you. I always figured you'd do the same for me."

Ethan cocked his head. "You know I would, but what's that got to do with a fellow thinking you're an heiress?"

"Heiress?" She slapped her thigh and tilted her head back in a boisterous laugh. "I thought you said airhead."

As tempting an opening for a barb as that was, Ethan let it pass. The banter would have to wait for a time when they weren't under such close scrutiny.

The waitress came by to hand Felicia a white take-out container and Ethan the check. Felicia slid the remainder of her steak and her untouched slices of toast into the container and closed it. Ethan whisked a bill from his wallet and laid it on the counter, telling the waitress, "Keep it."

He took Felicia's arm to help guide her toward the door, leaning close as he did and whispering, "Check your makeup."

"I'm not wearing any makeup."

"Then check to see if your nose is still out of joint," he commanded in a hushed voice.

"What?" She tried to tug her arm from his grasp.

He held firm. "Don't argue. Just take your mirror out of your purse and hold it up. That way we can see if we're being followed."

"Oh." She obeyed without further comment.

"Damn," Ethan muttered. He tipped his head slightly to indicate the reflection of the man a few paces behind them. "Just as I thought. He's not giving up that easily."

Felicia paused beside him just inside the restaurant door and cast her trusting gaze up at him. "What do we do now?"

"We're going to have to carry our ruse out a little longer." He pushed open the door and held it so she could walk past. "See those four eighteen-wheelers parked over there?"

She lowered her sunglasses to stare at the far end of the parking lot, then nodded.

"We'll head over there."

She matched his stride but her tone showed reluctance as she said, "What good will this do? We can't steal one of those huge trucks."

"No, but we can hide behind one, then wait for a break and dash back to our car."

They reached the trucks. When they had ducked between two of the gleaming giants, Felicia spun to face him. She extended her arms. "*This* is your plan?"

He crossed his arms over his chest. "You got a better one?"

Beside them, the door of a truck swung open and a startled trucker gawked down on them. A slow smile crept over Felicia's face. "As a matter of fact, I *do* have a better plan."

Ethan drew in a deep breath, ignoring the peculiar smell of oil, gasoline and diesel engine fumes. He hated to ask, but since his strategy was decidedly lacking, he had no choice. "So, you think you've got the solution to our predicament, huh?"

"You darn betcha." Felicia pulled her small shoulders up in a mingling of smugness and exuberance that Ethan found strangely enticing.

He bent forward to put himself nose to nose with her, savoring the closeness. He narrowed his eyes in an attempt to look tough, but when his gaze met hers, he knew he would fail. He felt a soft grin tug at his lips and he whispered, "This is your chance, Miss High Horse. Dazzle me."

Chapter Seven

"Admit it." Felicia ran both hands through her hair, trying to fluff up the curls that had been squashed by the blue cap. She practically bounced in the passenger seat of the rental car. "Admit it was a brilliant idea."

"That," Ethan said through his teeth, "was just the same old stunt you've tried to pull again and again ever since we hooked up for this fiasco."

She slumped down, feeling her enthusiasm deflate like a pricked balloon.

"Only, this time, it worked." He revved the engine as he guided the car over the bumpy road leading to their campsite. "In fact, your tired old gambit may have just saved our behinds, Miss High Horse."

Brightness flooded again into her being. She felt it radiate in her smile as she turned to Ethan. "Do you really think so?"

"We're here, aren't we? And as far as I can tell, we don't have any company." His gaze shifted upward to the rearview mirror. "Nope. No one following us."

"So, then, you're admitting that my idea, to pay one trucker to put on my cap and drive us to the highway, and another to meet us there in this car, was brilliant?"

Ethan pulled up beside their camper and parked the car. "I don't think I'd go so far as to call it brilliant. Expensive might be a more apt description."

Felicia watched him pull his wallet from his back pocket. He flipped it open and thumbed the thin collection of bills inside. She tried to look disinterested while, from the corner of her eye, she checked the contents of the dark leather wallet. No pictures. No keepsakes. Only a couple of worn credit cards and some cash. She didn't know whether to feel elated that he didn't carry some woman's photo or disheartened to find no intriguing clues to the inner workings of Ethan Bradshaw.

"Bad news," he said, folding the wallet shut. "I'm down to about eight dollars and change."

"You're worried about money?" She rolled her eyes and laughed aloud.

"Well, excuse me, princess, but some of us do have to think about money from time to time." He pushed the car door open with his shoulder and got out.

"That's not what I—" A thunderous slam cut her off.

Now she'd done it. Why couldn't she use enough foresight in dealing with Ethan to know when to keep her mouth shut? Or, at the very least, to weigh her words before she just blurted them out? He'd never believe she hadn't been speaking as a snobbish heiress now. She clenched her teeth, staring after him as he walked around the camper, pretending to inspect it for who knew what.

And he had accused *her* of hardheadedness and pride. She blew out a huff of air. He'd often displayed both those uncharming attributes in the many years she'd known him.

She'd only been seven when her mother had died and her father had decided the best place to raise a child alone was a thousand-acre dirt patch in Texas. Ethan and his daddy had come calling right away. The elder Bradshaw had wanted to extend a welcome and offer condolences. After all, he had said, he understood the trials of a widower raising a child, his own wife had died a few years earlier. Mr. Bradshaw suggested that the two families might get together for barbecues and so forth. And in emergencies, Bradshaw had said, his teenage son would be available to watch over the Grantham child. Just their way of being good neighbors, he had added. And Ethan, although clearly not overjoyed at the prospect, told her he'd looked after his sister's children. Then he'd reached out to pat her on the head.

And how had she and her father responded to the Texas hospitality? Her father had seen fit to explain that his daughter was always adequately cared for and he wouldn't need the Bradshaws' help, as though the man had just asked for a job. Then she'd kicked Ethan hard in the shins and run off screaming. To top off the melee, her father had stood right there and made an offer for the Bradshaw spread.

Felicia shook her head. No wonder the Bradshaws and the Granthams never could get along. Still, she had to smile at the sweet irony of life. All those years ago, her father had declined Ethan's services. And when she had sought to escape her father's tyranny, whom had she turned to? She jerked her head up. There sat Ethan sulking on the camper steps.

Warmth permeated her chest as she watched him sit with his arms on his knees, staring directly ahead, a stony glint in his eyes. Oh, how she knew that look.

"Please, Ethan, teach me how to ride a horse," she could hear herself saying it just as clearly as if it were today and not a summer nineteen years ago. She'd been twelve and Ethan was home from college. She thought he was the smartest, bravest, most interesting individual on earth. And she would do anything just to be near him. He showed a passing tolerance for her adoration but when he'd had enough...

She glanced again at the solitary figure with the sullen face and she smiled.

Of course, she much preferred Ethan's withdrawal to the rejection she suffered at his hands shortly after her sixteenth birthday. Felicia raised one knee up and hugged it as her thoughts drifted back. Ethan had returned for his first visit in a long while. His father had been so proud, telling everyone who would listen about Ethan's job on a first-class newspaper.

But even she could sense the tension between the Bradshaw men. Now she realized it was because the older man had begun selling off tracts of Bradshaw land to her father—because neither Ethan nor his older sister wanted the burden of the struggling ranch. Ethan had blamed her father for the loss of the family land, accusing him of exerting undo pressure on his ailing father.

She bit her lower lip and sighed. Maybe if Ethan hadn't harbored so much animosity for her father, things would have gone differently that day. She shut her eyes and the whole scene began to play out vividly in her mind.

"It's so sweet of you to teach me how to take pictures, Ethan," she had said in a young girl's version of a breathy whisper.

"Yeah, well, I wanted to get a few photos of this spot, and since it's now on Grantham land, I guess it's only right I let you tag along," he had grumbled.

Ethan had just taken her hand to help her out of his daddy's beat-up pickup truck when she saw her advantage and decided to use it. She stood on the old truck's running board, every fiber of her being alive with the knowledge that this placed her young breasts at Ethan's eye level. She pretended to stretch her back, thrusting her chest out in true teen-nymph style.

The pale blue of Ethan's eyes decreased as his pupils dilated. He wet his lips as though he were parched.

The subtle attention set her skin tingling and egged her on. She braced her free hand against his broad shoulder and leaned toward him, her lips poised to meet his.

He shut his eyes. A strange, primal moan eased up from deep in his chest. The sound startled and excited Felicia. Two centimeters closer and she would be kissing the sexiest man alive.

Felicia hesitated and in that moment gave Ethan the chance to reconsider.

He put his hands on her shoulders to steady her, then stepped back. "No."

The single word rang like a slap in the quiet of the summer day. "No? What do you mean, no?"

"I mean, this is wrong. I'm a grown man and you're just a kid." He released her and took up his camera.

She jumped down from the truck's running board to follow behind him. "I'm not a kid. I'm old enough to know what I want."

"And not old enough to know when you shouldn't try to get it." Ethan raised his camera and began adjusting the lens.

"But..."

"End of discussion, Miss High Horse."

"How dare you call me that."

"It suited you eight years ago and it suits you now." He shrugged. "Now, can you quiet down? I came out here to get some pictures."

She maneuvered around in front of him. "And I came out here to be alone with you, Ethan Bradshaw."

He lowered the camera.

"What did you think? That I wanted to learn how to take pictures?" she ranted, her hands on her hips. "I'm Felicia Grantham. If I want a picture taken, I can hire a legion of top professional photographers to take it for me. I don't need lessons from a hack reporter with a camera he still owes five payments on."

"Well, well, I see you inherited some of the famous Grantham charm." He raised the camera again. "Step aside, please. You're blocking my shot."

She crossed her arms under her breasts, making sure she accentuated her assets in the process. "Are you saying you don't think I'm beautiful?"

"Oh, I fully appreciate how beautiful you are." He snapped a picture of the landscape, then lowered the camera. "But I also think fire and rattlesnakes are beautiful, and I'm smart enough to keep a respectable distance from them, too."

The iciness in his eyes made her shiver but the heat of her longing for Ethan Bradshaw would not let her waver. "I don't want you to keep a respectable distance from me. And if it's respect you're worried about, if you're afraid my father will cause trouble because you're not my social equal..."

He seized her by the shoulders, not roughly, but with an intensity of purpose that stilled the words in her throat. Her legs weakened, threatening to fail her completely. He pulled her to him. As though propelled by a greater force, her body fit to his, closer still than he had brought her. His gaze, his scent, his warmth filled her. She tipped her head back, her lips parted, waiting.

"Get this straight, little girl," Ethan said through teeth clenched so tight, his cheek looked like taut leather. "I am not now, nor will I ever be, afraid of your father—for any reason. Understand?"

She swallowed, then nodded.

"And as for my worrying about showing the Granthams the proper respect?"

"Yes?" Her whisper crackled like a dry twig underfoot.

She could only compare the sparkle in his eyes to diamonds—since she had never seen anything more breathtaking yet so hard.

He let her go, stepping backward as he did. Forever in her mind she would remember the image of him retreating from her, his head lifted in a howl of laughter.

Felicia choked back a soft sob. When she opened her eyes, she was surprised to find a tear on her cheek. She stared from her seat in the car at the man who had hurt and humiliated her all those years ago.

Did he realize, she wondered, how strongly that had affected her? Did he know that from that day forward she used the pretense of superiority to keep people at bay? Oh, she couldn't blame Ethan for her reluctance to trust or her aversion to giving control over to anyone. Her father had laid the groundwork for those traits long before. Still, Ethan's behavior that summer day survived in her mind as the perfect example of why she had to maintain the upper hand with all men.

She watched him stub the toe of his boot in the dust like a pouting eight-year-old, and she couldn't help smiling again at the ironic twist life had taken. No man other than Ethan could have gone so far in breaching those very barriers he helped create so long ago. In the past few days she'd trusted him more, listened to him more and given in to him more than any other man in her life. Though she hadn't done it very graciously.

She undid her safety belt and hopped out of the car. This was her chance to make up for a little of the aggravation she'd caused him.

"Tell you what I'm gonna do," she called in the style of a carnival barker. "I'm prepared to offer you the opportunity of a lifetime."

Ethan looked up, the perplexed anticipation in his eyes at odds with the frown on his thin lips.

"You, yes, you, sir," she went on, walking toward him, "are about to be treated like royalty."

He raised his eyebrows to question her statement.

"Yes, royalty." She waved her arms in a grand flourish. "An aristocrat of the highest regard. A sovereign of stratospheric supremacy."

He chuckled.

"A king." She stopped just at his feet. "His Majesty. The Big Cheese."

"Is that so?"

"That, sir, is so." She nodded once to affirm her own words. "And what, you may ask yourself, will this cost me?"

"So we're back to money, huh?" Only an edge in his voice betrayed the anger he had shown earlier. But even that dispelled when he finished. "It had better be less than eight dollars."

"I assure you, you won't pay eight dollars. Not seven dollars, not even five dollars. In fact, this won't cost you one red cent. Now what do you say about that?"

"I say, what are you up to, Miss High Horse?"

"I'm up to the task at hand, Bradshaw," she replied in her normal tone. "Namely, packing up our campsite so we can get back on our way to Vegas."

"Vegas?" He cocked his head.

"Yeah, Vegas." She shifted her weight and crossed her arms. "Maybe you've heard of it? Flashy city in the desert? Gambler's Paradise? Sin City?" She waggled her eyebrows at him. "Last I heard, we were headed there to reunite me with a certain Todd Armstrong."

A heavy rush of breath blew through Ethan's pursed lips as he rose from the camper's steps. His grave eyes never blinked as he looked down on her and said, "Last I heard, a certain Todd Armstrong wasn't going anywhere—and coincidentally, neither are we."

"I beg your pardon?"

"No need to beg, princess, I'll be happy to explain it so you can understand." Ethan felt his grin stretch as Felicia's expression changed from smugness to indignance. Lucky for him she didn't have anything handy to throw or he'd be nursing a bump on his head for sure. He held his hands up to quell her response while he launched his explanation. "You said Armstrong lives in Las Vegas, right?"

"Right."

"And that you expect him to be there whenever you can get to him?"

She jerked her chin up, the rose color draining from her tightening lips. "As long as it's a reasonable amount of time, yes."

Ethan laid his hand on his chest and groaned out a phony sigh. "Even true love has its limits, I suppose."

"Forget true love, Bradshaw. *I* have *my* limits and you're pushing them."

Good, he thought. He liked pushing her. He liked seeing her reach beyond that spoiled debutante persona and act like a real woman. He liked seeing passion flare in her eyes. He'd like it more under other circumstances, but he'd enjoy this small dose of pleasure while he could. "Put aside your impatience to get to Armstrong for half a second, Felicia, and think."

"I am thinking," she insisted at top volume. As if to verify that statement, she scowled and stared toward the pine trees directly behind the camper. After a moment, she turned her exasperated expression on him. "Just what am I supposed to be thinking about?"

"About what happened at the truck stop," he prodded.

"Um, we ate. And we ran away from…" She glanced up at him, all tension evaporated from her features. "Someone knows we're in the vicinity."

"Now you're cooking." He stepped up to place a hand on her shoulder. "And?"

"And that man may just be one of many."

"And?"

"And since Todd will be waiting, for a while at least…"

He nodded to coax the solution from her.

"We have time to come up with another plan to get us to Vegas."

"Yes!" He laid his open hand out to her.

She blinked down at the common gesture.

Ethan's expectations sank again. No matter how good a sport she was, or how much of the real person he could bring out in Felicia, she could never be anything but what she was: a society princess. Just as he started to let his offered hand drop, a sharp stinging filled his palm. He glanced at her, stunned.

When she extended her own open hand for him to slap in congratulations, he chuckled and obliged.

"We may make a regular human being out of you yet, Miss High Horse," he teased.

"And when we're finished with me, we'll get to work on you," she shot back with a twinkle in her dark eyes. "Though turning you into a human being may be a little too ambitious. Maybe we can get you to act more like a whole donkey instead of just the hind quarters. What do you say to that?"

"Hee-haw," he brayed at the top of his lungs.

She joined him in a laugh for a moment, but when they settled down, she was all business. "Okay, we need to get serious now. We need to come up with some alternatives to our original plan to get to Vegas."

"I thought we'd lay low here until dark." He twisted his shoulders to survey the campgrounds. "It's quiet and secluded and no one knows us."

Felicia nodded. "Good idea. Then we'll do our driving at night?"

"Be a lot harder to spot us then, don't you think?"

"Yes." She bit her lip and patted her tennis shoe on the softly packed dirt. "It really makes sense to do it that way. How much time will it add to the trip?"

Jealousy at her eagerness to reach her husband-to-be stabbed at Ethan's ego. He forced himself to ignore the nonproductive emotion. "It won't add any more actual drive time, of course. But we sure won't be rolling into Vegas tonight."

"Sometime tomorrow night, then?"

Yeah, you'll be in Loverboy's arms tomorrow night, he thought. A burning bitterness rose in his gullet. Felicia might even be Mrs. Todd Armstrong before dawn two days from now. He turned his back to her to keep his face or his tone from betraying his distaste for the future he had promised to help her realize. "Yeah, we'll probably be there tomorrow night. That okay by you?"

"Fine. And, Ethan?"

He was startled to feel her small hand on his arm. He wanted to envelop that hand with his own. He wanted to take her in his arms and kiss all thoughts of her beefcake boyfriend out of her mind forever. And then what? Would he whisk her off to his sun-baked dirt plot in Texas to live in the lap of mediocrity? He glanced down at the delicate hand curved over his forearm. He couldn't imagine it blistered by the hard work of building a home. He raised his gaze to her lovely face. That was not the face of a woman destined to live the quiet family life far from fame and excitement—and most modern conveniences.

"Ethan?" she asked again in that rich, angelic tone she used much too rarely.

"Hmm?"

"I want you to know I appreciate the way you handled things this time. I don't suppose you can know how much it means to me."

"What?"

"To be asked what I think, silly. To be included in the planning instead of told what to do and when to do it." She smiled at him. "I thought you'd done that on purpose, but your reaction tells me differently."

Quiet dread welled within him. He winced in anticipation of the verbal punishment he expected to follow. "Go ahead, take your best shot. Lambaste me for doing the right thing for the wrong reason."

A bell-like peal of laughter answered him. "I'm not mad, just the opposite, in fact."

Ethan could only shake his head. "You baffle me, Miss High—Felicia. Are you saying you're glad I stumbled into involving you in the planning?"

Her smile beamed brighter still. "I'm glad it wasn't a calculated move on your part. It shows a change in your attitude. A subtle change, I admit."

"Yeah, so subtle, I didn't even realize it."

She lifted her eyebrows and tossed back her thick black hair. "Who knows? I may make you into a human after all." She winked, then spun on her heel, calling back, "At the very least, there's no doubt that I am having some effect on you."

Ethan's gaze followed the swing of her hips as she sashayed away from him. His blood pulsed to that slow sensuous rhythm. He tried to swallow but couldn't; his chest and his blue jeans had both suddenly become tight and constricting. He forced a long blast of warm air out of his lungs and shook his head again. "Oh, no doubt about that at all, Miss High Horse. You *still* have an effect on me. I only hope I survive the next two days without doing something about it."

Chapter Eight

"This assignment will be the death of me yet," Ethan muttered, glancing around the convenience store to make sure Felicia could not hear him from where she waited by the ladies' room. Gripping the receiver of the pay phone mounted on the back wall, Ethan deposited most of his stash of quarters and dialed his ex-boss.

"Give me Bob Harding," Ethan directed the voice that answered. "Bob? It's Ethan."

"Where the hell are you hiding and how long can you stay there?"

Ethan chuckled at the gruff greeting. "I'm fine, and you?"

"I'll be just dandy if you tell me you can stretch this story out for all its worth."

"Stretch it?" The suggestion wedged like a hot coal in Ethan's chest. "Are you nuts? I was calling to say we could wrap it up early tomorrow night."

"No can do." It was more of a command than a comment. "This is too good. You've got the whole country watching and wondering what happened to your little friend. Every hour you prolong the wait, the ratings go up."

"It's too chancy, Bob," Ethan argued. "We almost got caught today."

"But obviously you didn't."

"Yeah, but..."

"But nothing. This is kid's play for a reporter like you, Bradshaw."

"Let me tell you, this is anything but kid's play, pal. You don't have the whole story on this girl."

"What?" the other man barked. "That she's a hot-blooded handful? That you two practically grew up together? That your two families have a long-standing feud?"

That hot coal in his chest plummeted to his stomach. "You know all that?"

"Know it? We've been playing it as an angle in our paper."

"But how did you...?"

"That's our job, buddy," his ex-boss explained with a hard-bitten laugh. "And once her old man announced he thought she'd taken up with you, we moved on it. And is the public ever eating it up."

"They are?"

"Of course they are. There's even a faction betting you've whisked the Grantham girl off for yourself."

"That's ridiculous," Ethan said through clenched teeth, wishing he were in a more private spot so he could underscore his sentiment with a few well-placed curses.

"Ridiculous, eh? Too bad. It would have made blockbuster copy."

"I'm not in the business of making the news, Bob. I only report it."

"And photograph it. We need pictures, boy, lots of pictures."

"Yeah, yeah."

"Well, if that's all you wanted..."

"Wait." Ethan held his hand out as though Bob could see the gesture from his office hundreds of miles away. "That's not all. I'm going to need some cash, Bob."

"How much, where and when?"

Ethan blinked at the black pay phone as if it had suddenly malfunctioned. "That was too easy."

"Look, if laying out a few bucks keeps this story going, it's worth it. Now, what arrangements can we make?"

"Let's see." Ethan sighed and rubbed the back of his neck. "We're only traveling at night, so as soon as we get settled tomorrow morning, I'll call you and you can have someone bring it to me then. We shouldn't be too far out of Vegas."

Silence answered him.

"Bob? Are you still there?"

"Nope. I'm one day in the future."

"Huh?"

"I'm envisioning tomorrow's headline."

Ethan shut his eyes and placed his forehead against the painted wall beside the phone. "What do you have up your permanently ink-stained sleeve, Bob?"

"You said you were only traveling by night, right?"

Ethan curled his fingers more tightly around the smooth receiver. "So?"

"So, how's this grab you? The Midnight Ride of the Fugitive Bride."

Ethan groaned.

"Like it or not, it's going to sell papers."

Ethan wanted to argue, but just as he opened his mouth, Felicia emerged from the recessed area where the rest rooms were located. "Look, Bob, I have to go. I'll call again in the morning."

He slammed the receiver down and called out to Felicia, but she ducked her head and rushed toward the door.

Felicia rubbed her burning eyes and wished it were daylight so she could slip on a pair of sunglasses. Instead, she blinked to chase away the bleariness, then squared her shoulders. She waved to Ethan and pushed open the heavy glass door, singsonging with excessive cheeriness, "I'm heading out to the car. Will you be long?"

"I just have to freshen up," he joked. "Do you want to pick up a snack or—"

"No thanks." She pushed her way outside. The cool night breeze nipped her cheeks and nose. She took a deep breath to pull the cleansing cold inside her lungs. Despite the smell of gasoline and oil, she welcomed the rush of air.

"Felicia?" The store door fell shut with a whoosh while Ethan's footsteps scuffed over the pavement. "Felicia, are you all right?"

She froze. "Me? I'm fine. Why do you ask?"

He came up behind her, so close, she thought she could feel the stiffness of his denim jacket through the two T-shirts she wore.

"Look at me," he demanded.

"Why would I want to do that?" she asked with forced snideness.

"Look at me." This time it was more of a request.

She turned slowly to look up into his concern-ridden face.

"You've been crying."

She started to shake her head, paused, then let it fall into a nod as heavy as her heart.

"Why? Did somebody say something?" He gripped her upper arms and bent at the knees to bring his eyes level to hers. "Did they do something to upset you?"

Again she nodded wearily.

"Who was it?" He glanced back at the brightly lit store, his eyes darting back and forth to seek out the culprit. "What did they do? Tell me and I'll go in there and—"

"Nobody *did* anything to me, Ethan."

"Then someone said something? There's no need for you to just accept insults, either, Felicia."

"Except from you, of course," she said.

"Yeah, well, that goes without saying." He cleared his throat.

Amusement and satisfaction at ribbing Ethan lifted her spirits enough to allow her to recount what had happened.

"Oh, Ethan," she began, a sigh causing her voice to shudder. "I've been so sheltered. I've seen more of the real world in the past two days than in two decades."

"What are you talking about, Felicia?" He draped his sturdy, comforting arm over her shoulders and walked her toward the car.

She leaned back to rest against the fender. "When I was waiting for the rest room, I met a woman with the saddest story."

Ethan pressed his hand to the roof of the car, bracing his arm straight beside Felicia's head. "You mean some woman hanging around outside a rest room told you a sob story and you believed it?"

"It wasn't a sob story and yes, I believed her," she said with bristling impatience. "Now, do you want to hear this or do you want to carry on like a couple of warring wildcats?''

Ethan's lips quirked into a mischievous half smile. ''Much as I like that wildcat thing, I have the feeling the correct answer is A. Tell your story.''

She shut her eyes for a moment to still the emotional turmoil that her recent experience had caused. When she opened them again, she focused her gaze on the blur of color and movement inside the convenience store.

''As I said, I met this woman. She looked to be about my age....''

''That old, huh?''

Despite her dark mood, a spark of laughter overtook Felicia. Still, she managed to chastise Ethan with a scowl. ''The woman looked to be about my age and she had two children with her. A toddler—at least I think that's what they call them...''

''About yea high?'' Ethan held his hand out around knee-level. ''Not talking too much yet? Could hardly keep still?''

Felicia nodded in stunned admiration. ''I had no idea you knew so much about children.''

''Hey, I happen to know plenty...of people who have children.''

She rolled her gaze upward. The unnatural glow of the overhead lights immediately stung her eyes. Blinking, she lowered her head and went on with the tale. ''Anyway, she had this toddler and a baby.''

''A baby.''

She chose not to play to the obnoxious overemphasis he put on the word. ''A very sweet baby,'' she confirmed quietly. ''In fact, she let me go ahead of her in line because she needed to use the ladies' room to give the children a quick bath. She knew that would take a while.''

"A bath? In a rest room?"

That hooked him, she thought. Maybe now he wouldn't be so smug and judgmental about the woman's unfortunate situation. "Yes, it seems she was living out of her car for the time being."

"Homeless?"

"Not exactly homeless, more like hotelless."

"Uh-oh."

"What does that mean?"

"Nothing," he said, his features blank. "Go on."

Felicia watched him for a second, wondering whether to pursue the needling remark. The buzz from the overhead lighting seemed to swell in the silence. She studied his face. Maybe someday she would look at that face and her heart would not skip. Maybe, years and years from now, she would not feel that primitive urge to tangle with him verbally to keep her emotional—and physical—distance. Yeah, and maybe she'd just sprout wings and fly herself to Las Vegas.

She shifted her weight and narrowed one eye at him in warning. "This woman was living out of her car because she was leaving her abusive husband in California and trying to get to her parents' home in Dallas. And she just hadn't realized how much money that would take."

She clamped her mouth shut and waited for Ethan to toss in a cynical observation. When none came, she continued. "She'd gotten so close. Then she checked her finances and decided she only had enough funds to pay for gas. The niceties like hotels and restaurants got cut from the travel budget."

"How much did you give her?" he asked flatly.

"Everything."

If they had been in a cartoon, Ethan's blue eyes would have shot lightning bolts. Steam would have billowed from under his collar. His face would have gone scarlet, then purple. Sirens would have gone off. As it was, his jaw clenched. Red spots warmed the hollow of his cheeks. He raised his hands, his fingers curled to rake through his shiny black hair. His eyes did bulge a little and his pupils grew wide, to give him that wild appearance. But no lightning. No steam.

When he spoke, it was with measured force. "You did what?"

"I gave her all my money," Felicia repeated slowly. "Except for my change."

Ethan straightened away from the car and pinched the bridge of his nose, his eyes shut. "How much change?"

"Why could that possibly matter?"

"Because that change and the precious little cash I've got is all we have to get us to Vegas, my dear."

"Oh, Ethan." She put her hand on her stomach and laughed, as much in relief as in humor. "That's ridiculous. I have tons of money."

"Where?"

"What do you mean where? In the bank. I also have a very diverse portfolio." She crossed her arms over her chest. "There are even rumors of a secret Swiss bank account."

"Might as well all be in Switzerland for all the good it will do us," Ethan muttered, mirroring her stance.

She glanced from the muscular arms folded over his broad chest to his taut face. The smallest seed of alarm caused her voice to thin as she asked, "What do you mean by that?"

"Well, how did you plan to get your hands on your money?"

Relief flooded over her. "There's this great big money machine, see?" She made a bold gesture as though pantomiming for a child. "And I take this itty-bitty plastic card and feed it to the big old machine."

"Which promptly enters the data into a big ol' computer system that records all vital information, like who you are and where you made your withdrawal. Remember when you tried to use your credit card in Smokewater?"

"Oh." How could she have been so foolish not to think of that? She met Ethan's hard gaze and imagined seeing herself shrinking in his estimation.

"Didn't you realize that your bank would be watching your account?" he asked.

She drew herself up to her full height. "Why would they? I'm not a criminal, you know."

"I know, but as far as the authorities are concerned, you are a missing person. Until they rule out foul play, they'll be watching for something just like a cash withdrawal from your account."

"Or at the very least, my father will have discovered some weasel at the bank willing to tip him off in exchange for a hefty bonus."

"You don't paint a very pretty picture of your father," Ethan said, his eyes narrowed.

"It's not him. It's the money." All the gains she'd made with Ethan seemed to be fading in the wake of this one action. He hadn't complained about her father in quite a while. Not to mention that he'd begun to treat her as a competent person. But now...

She cast her gaze down and wound one finger in a coil of black hair. "Money changes people—changes the way they act toward those who have it. Sometimes it leads people to challenge their loyalties."

"And your father takes advantage of that."

Felicia fought back a shudder and sighed. "My father is a good man. But he's an even better businessman. And he has been a terrific father."

"Then why are you running away from him?"

"Am I?" She pushed away from the car's fender, walked a few steps toward the store, then pivoted back to Ethan. "I know it sounds corny, but I like to think I'm running toward something."

Ethan stiffened. The light in his eyes dimmed.

Felicia would bet what little money she had left that he assumed she meant she was running to Todd. If there were one single reason to tell him the truth, she would. But given that after they reached Vegas, she would never see Ethan Bradshaw again, it all seemed so pointless. She shrugged. "So, are we dead in the water, or can we make it to Vegas?"

"Well, the tank is over half full. We should be able to get pretty far on that—if we unhitch the trailer and leave it behind."

"Leave it? But where will we sleep?"

"When we stop in the morning, I've arranged for someone to bring out some cash...."

"Hold it right there, buster. You say you've already made plans to get more money?" Her posture relayed her annoyance as much as her tone. "Then how dare you lecture me about giving my money away."

"How dare I?" He stood up to her, toe to toe, bending his neck to make his gaze meet hers. "You had no way of knowing I could get more money. You didn't stop to think anything through. That could have gotten us both in a hell of a lot of hot water."

"Have you taken a whiff of us lately, Bradshaw?" She turned her head and raised her nose into the breeze. "We could both stand a little hot water—and some soap."

Tiny crinkles spread from the corners of his smiling eyes to his tanned cheeks. "You'll be the death of me yet, do you know that, Miss High Horse?"

"A girl can dream. Now, you were about to tell me where we were going to sleep without the camper."

"After I get an infusion of cash, we'll get a motel."

"A motel?" She clasped her hands high across her chest. "With my very own private shower?"

"Yeah, I think we can arrange that." He stepped close to put his hand under her chin. "But until then it'll mean tightening our belts—literally. I don't think we can afford anything more than a soda and a candy bar to eat all night."

Much as she wanted to simply savor the feel of his hand on her skin, she took her chin from his palm and gazed with determination into his eyes. "I can do it, Ethan."

"I have no doubt you can." He shook his head.

"Really?" She gulped down some air, gas station fumes and all. "The way you talked a moment ago, I thought you'd lost all your hard-won faith in me."

He smiled. The harsh outdoor lighting accentuated the lines around his eyes, the creases framing his pale lips.

"Anyone can make a mistake," he said, reaching out to stroke his thumb down her cheek. "Even Miss High Horse."

She turned her face to his hand, whispering into his rough palm, "I should have thought about not being able to access my bank account, yes. But I don't believe that giving that poor woman my money was a mistake."

He caressed her cheek, then smoothed his hand down to rest against her neck. "You really are the naive one, Felicia."

She raised her shoulder to prevent him from withdrawing his hand, relishing the skin-to-skin contact. Touch me more, touch me everywhere, her senses cried. Images of Ethan holding her naked body to his came unbidden to her mind. She struggled to banish them, wondering how naive he would think her if he knew the lusty thoughts his touch evoked in her.

"That woman might very well have just scammed you," he continued. "It happened before, you know."

His scolding words snapped her out of her sensual reverie. "So I gave that Drake fellow five hundred dollars in Smokewater. Don't you think I feel miserable enough about that now?"

"You mean because you're broke?"

It was a good thing that Ethan's hand lay on her neck and not the other way around. Otherwise, she would have slapped him senseless. "No, not because I'm broke. Do you really think I'm that shallow?"

"Did I say you were shallow?"

"When you implied that I only wanted that lost money for my own personal comfort, you did. Didn't it occur to you that I might dislike injustice, just like you 'normal' people? Did you ever think I might wish I had that money back so I would have had more to give to that lady and her children?"

"You're kidding."

"I am not."

He shook his head. "I never pegged you for the type to fall so easily for a tragic tale from a stranger."

"And what type did you have me pegged for?" Her blood raced as did her mind, pouring passion into her speech as she rushed on. "The type who could listen to that kind of story, who could look into the eyes of a hungry child and do nothing?"

"What if it was a con job?"

"What if it was? I believed it was true and that's enough. I couldn't respect myself if I'd walked away without helping. If you can't respect me for that, then maybe we should end our alliance."

She jerked her head up, hoping that would keep the tears from spilling onto her cheeks. She summoned the last of her outrage to offer what she hoped he would not accept. "I have enough change left to make a phone call. If you really think so little of me, do us both a favor and let me use it."

She held her breath and watched, waiting. The glaring overhead lights emphasized the contrast of Ethan's coloring, making his teeth whiter, his hair blacker and his eyes so blue, they shimmered. Felicia shivered at the intensity of the effect.

"Here." He slid the denim jacket from his shoulders and laid it over hers. "I still need to make a trip inside. Why don't you get in the car. It's warmer there."

The tightness in his tone and the softness of his demeanor were sufficient to dissuade Felicia from making the call. She snuggled into the warm jacket and drew in Ethan's lingering scent. She answered the anxiety in his eyes with a nod and a smile.

When he had helped her into the car, he turned and headed back inside the store.

What the hell was wrong with him? He had his chance to get rid of her and he blew it. To make matters worse, he'd all but committed himself to his ex-boss to prolong their rabid adventure as long as possible.

Seeing there was a short line outside the men's room, Ethan strode over to the soda case and stared blankly at the rows of cans and bottles. What was he thinking? It wasn't as though he had anything to gain from all this nonsense.

Sure, he thought, there was his so-called revenge on Gower Grantham. He rubbed his hand up the back of his neck. The movement caused him to notice his own reflection in the glass doors. The sight startled him and made him a little uncomfortable. Who was he to seek revenge from anyone anyway?'

Like he was such a saint. He glanced at his faded flannel shirt, then pretended to smooth down his shaggy black hair. He didn't look himself in the face. How could he? He'd been so quick to condemn Gower Grantham for buying up his family's land. Yet when Ethan experienced professional burnout, had he balked at using the inheritance the sale of the land provided?

And what about that journalistic integrity he produced when it suited him? Telling Bob Harding he didn't make the news when that was his plan all along—to create a sensation and use it to humiliate Gower Grantham. He hung his head.

The whole idea seemed sour now. Hurting someone Felicia loved, compromising his ideals in the process, and for what? He didn't need the money and he couldn't get the girl.

He craned his neck to peer outside at the car. Felicia sat with her back to the passenger door. Her head lay against the glass, her black hair cascading over her shoulders. Even though that was all he could see of her, the sight thrilled him. It roused his senses, calling him to go to her and bury a thousand kisses in that hair. To pull her to him and never let go.

He grit his teeth and felt the tension in his jaw stretch all the way down his body. That's why he hadn't let her make the phone call. It's why he hadn't called the whole farce off himself. He wanted her too badly. He wasn't ready to end their relationship—in whatever form it took.

Was that worth the pain of knowing he was taking the one woman who could challenge him mentally, best him verbally and still make his body ache with desire, to marry another man?

Felicia shifted in the car to put her face in profile. The vision lifted more than Ethan's spirits.

Yes, he decided, it was worth every agonizing second he could eke out of the situation.

Chapter Nine

"I hate being hungry." Felicia eyed the vending machines at the rest stop. Her stomach grumbled. "I can't believe we don't even have enough to get a bag of peanuts or something."

"Sorry, but that package of gum you had to have a couple of hours ago broke the bank." Ethan slicked his hair back with one hand and scratched at his day-old beard with the other. "Don't worry, though. Bob's messenger should be here with some money any minute."

"How will you recognize him?" she asked, trying desperately to keep up some form of casual conversation. Otherwise, her exhaustion, the close quarters and her attraction to Ethan might get the better of her.

Even now, when she saw him looking all bleary-eyed and scruffy, she thought he was the most virile man alive. It didn't help matters that she had pretended to sleep off and on through the night in order to enjoy the sound of him singing along with the radio. Or that she had cuddled beneath his denim jacket all that time, and now even her own T-shirt carried a soft hint of Ethan's masculine scent. She pressed her aching back to the slightly reclined car seat and sighed. "Ethan?"

"Hmm?"

"How will you recognize this messenger?"

"He'll be in one of the news bureau's vans." Ethan shifted in his seat and winced.

Obviously he was as tired of sitting as she was, Felicia thought. Her eyes drifted south of Ethan's beltline to the side view of his backside. She was too weary to keep herself from wondering...

"They're big and white and ugly as the dickens."

"Th-they are?" She batted her lashes to hide her astonishment at hearing the question in her mind answered aloud.

"Oh, yeah." He shut his eyes and rolled his neck against the headrest behind him. "They're beat-up like you wouldn't believe. And one of them has a bullet hole high on the left—"

"A bullet hole? You're kidding." She knew he'd lived a life of high adventure, but even she was surprised at this revelation. "I never suspected the news game could be so dangerous."

He laughed. "It can be, I suppose, but that scar wasn't earned in the line of duty. Someone was just in the wrong place at the wrong time. One of those 'I didn't know she was married' deals."

Felicia could feel her mouth hanging open but seemed powerless to close it. She tried to process the overload of information Ethan had thrown at her, concluding that his uncharacteristic forthrightness about himself sprang from fatigue.

"Anyway, that's neither here nor there," he said before she could formulate a response. "The best way to tell if it's one of our vans is..."

"Van?" she whispered, her lips tingling as the word blew past. Confusion and concern gave way to a release of buoyant laughter. Heat rose from her chest to her cheeks, and her empty stomach shook with a fit of giggles. "Oh, my gosh, you were talking about the vans."

"Uh-huh." His black brows slanted down over his bewildered blue eyes. "What did you *think* I was talking about?"

She sobered instantly, feeling her eyes widen as she stared at him and answered, "The vans. What else could it be?"

"I think someone is suffering from sleep deprivation."

"And don't forget food deprivation." She patted her stomach. "Let's see if we can spot that big white van."

She twisted in her seat, scanning the long parking lot of the rest stop. Her gaze swept over the small gravel picnic area in front of the yellow brick building that housed the rest rooms. To the left of the building stood a row of vending machines, to the right a sparse cactus garden. Even though it was barely past dawn, the place was bustling. She counted no less than a dozen eighteen-wheelers parked in a lot behind the rest stop building. The drivers were now stirring, emerging from the big rigs to stretch and pay a visit to the facilities. But she saw no vans, of any color.

She turned back to Ethan. "It's not over there." She jerked her head in the direction she had just searched. "You see it anywhere?"

He rubbed his eyes. "No."

She angled her shoulders toward Ethan, positioning herself to see out the back window. "Oh, look, there's a white van pulling into the lot now. That must be them."

"Good." Ethan tipped his head back to check in the rearview mirror.

Felicia pulled the door handle and started to get out.

"Whoa," Ethan barked. "Don't get out of the car."

"Why?" Even as she asked it, she shut the door.

"Take another look at that van." He narrowed his eyes, keeping them focused on the rectangular mirror. "Notice anything alarming?"

Felicia shrugged. "Just a typical white van with a TV news logo on the side."

He shifted his gaze to her face and cocked his head.

"Oh, my goodness." She swallowed. "That's not the van we're waiting for, is it?"

He shook his head.

"We're in one heck of a pickle, aren't we?"

He nodded.

She bit her lip and tried to regulate her breathing to prevent herself from getting too upset. "What are we going to do?"

"What can we do?" Ethan took the steering wheel in both hands and flexed his broad shoulders. "We can't run. We're almost out of gas. We have to meet our contact."

"How do you think they found us?"

"We don't know they're here for us." His clothes rasped against the car seat as he turned to face her. "But it's reasonable to assume that they won't leave us alone if they discover we are here."

"Then we have to make sure they don't discover us." She tugged at a stray curl dangling over her shoulder. "But how?"

"Just scrunch down in your seat." Ethan adjusted his body as best as he could to conceal his identity.

"Scrunch down? What good will that do?"

"It will keep us from drawing attention to ourselves."

"And what about your contact? Won't he draw attention to us?"

"Discretion is part of the job, Felicia. Whoever brings the money will simply stroll over and slip the envelope through the car window."

"Oh, that's brilliant. An unmarked van pulls into a roadside rest stop and a messenger jumps out and passes a package to two shady characters ducking down inside a rental car. That's the last thing that would pique a reporter's curiosity."

"You got a better idea?"

"I thought you'd never ask." She wiggled her eyebrows at him. "We have to waylay them."

His nose twitched. "Waylay?"

"Yes." She punched him lightly in the arm to punish him for teasing her over her choice of words. "Stall them, disable them, leave them in the dust."

"And how do you plan to do that?"

She opened her mouth to share the details but he held his hand up.

"Before you begin, remember that we don't have any money to pay anybody to detain these people." His lips lifted on one side and he narrowed one eye.

Drawing herself up to his self-satisfied challenge, she said, "Then we'll just have to do it ourselves. And if we should need some help?"

"Yes?" He crossed his arms.

"It's time you learned that money is not the only thing that motivates people to help others." She angled her chin up and gave him her brightest smile.

He chuckled. "Well, traveling with you has been an education, so there is hope for me yet."

"I think we've both learned some interesting lessons on this trip, Ethan." Impulsively, she leaned over and kissed his cheek. The second her lips touched his whiskered jaw, she regretted the action. A slow-burning tingle swept from the tip of her nose downward until her whole being shuddered with the urge to press against Ethan's body and lose herself in kiss after kiss.

With just a small shift of his head, Ethan brought his gaze to bore into hers. His mouth waited only centimeters from her own. Anticipation electrified the silence.

Not now, a voice in her befuddled brain managed to say. Not ever, her once-battered heart echoed. In the blink of an eye, she felt sixteen again and could see Ethan Bradshaw standing before her laughing at the fragile affection she offered. Just as quickly, the image evaporated.

She put her hands on his shoulders and pushed him lightly away. Bowing her head for a moment, she composed herself. "Um, as I was saying..."

"About your idea for handling the reporters," Ethan prompted.

Only the stunned glaze in his eyes told her he'd felt the power of what had almost happened. She shut her eyes to clear her head, then focused fully on the task at hand.

"First, we need a distraction," she said, taking charge.

"A distraction?" He scored his fingers down the length of his bristled cheek.

"You know, like they do on TV when they want to ensnare someone? They lure them away with a distraction." Exhilaration overtook exhaustion in her muscles, and she sat up, her hands waving in animated gestures. "Maybe a better word than distraction is *bait.*"

"Ensnare? Lure? Bait? Sounds like hunting season on reporters and you're setting a trap." He grimaced. "I'm not sure I like that, Felicia."

"What would you rather do? Sit there and watch your exclusive story get scooped?"

Ethan sat up. "You got me. You had to appeal to my sense of journalistic competition, but you got me. Now, what did you have in mind?"

Fifteen minutes later, Ethan flattened his back to the cold, rough brick of the rest stop's back wall. He leaned around the corner of the building, using a tall spiny cactus as cover while he watched for the two young men from the news van start back for it. He glowered at the cactus just inches from his nose and muttered, "I had to ask. I could have just insisted we do things my way. But no, I had to be Mr. Thoughtful and ask what she wanted to do."

"Shh." Felicia's arm swung full force into his stomach.

He pretended to double over at the blow and groaned.

"Will you hush?" she whispered. "You'll give us away."

"I can think of at least one of us I'd like to give away." He raised one eyebrow at her, forcing his gaze to remain on her face. Hardly an easy mission since she'd slipped into the filmy white belly dancer's costume she'd worn the night he'd rescued her on his land. "You realize, of course, that this can't work."

"It can and will work, if *we* do." She crossed her arms under her breasts. "Now, those nice truckers are waiting for my signal to move their rigs behind the news van and block it in. And I'm certainly ready to divert the two reporters long enough to let you slip inside their van and disable their cellular phone. The only potential fly in the ointment would be if your contact doesn't show up real soon."

"Actually, I think I see the van pulling in now." Ethan squinted between two prominent prickly plants at the entrance ramp into the rest area.

"Terrific." She grabbed his arm and gave it a squeeze. "After you get the money and take care of the phone, keep the car running so we can make a quick getaway."

He glanced down at her. The golden desert dawn washed over her breasts and bare midriff. The crisp spring air ruffled her shining black hair and the long silken scarves streaming from her headpiece. It brought her scent to him, even over the incessant fumes of cars and trucks. The gilded adornments on her costume clinked and flashed with even her slightest movement, drawing attention to every detail of her figure. He gulped down the rising wave of desire it all inspired and said, "I still don't get why you have to wear that outfit."

"We've been all through that, Ethan." She rolled her eyes and shook her head. "If they aren't already looking for us, we don't want to point ourselves out. Thanks to this costume and a well-placed veil, they may not notice who I am."

She whisked a length of sheer fabric across the lower half of her face and tucked it behind her ear. Lowering her chin, she gazed up at him from beneath her thick sooty lashes.

He could actually hear his pulse quicken. If he intended any witty critique of the image she presented, he forgot it.

"And," she went on with a sly smile, "if they should try to get too close a peak at my face..."

She rolled her hips in a slow, seductive figure eight that ended with an exuberant shinny. Above the sound of the costume's jingling, she asked, "Distracting enough?"

Language failed him. All coherent thought escaped his feeble brain. He coughed to clear the dryness from his throat and tugged at the waistband of his suddenly snug jeans. He opened his mouth, then simply nodded to her in silence.

"Good," she said. She slapped him hard on the back, adding a forward shove. "Now go out there and do what you have to do."

Do what you have to do. She would never have said that to him if she'd only known what he was thinking he had to do right now. His boots felt lined with lead as he trudged over to the white van where his contact waited.

"Why her?" he muttered to himself. Of all the women on earth, or even just the many who had shown interest in him, why did he have to have this chemistry with Felicia Grantham?

Chemistry? He shook his head. It went way beyond that. If inexplicable sexual attraction was called chemistry, then what he felt for Felicia could only be labeled alchemy—the changing of something common into something precious.

He'd felt it years ago when she was only sixteen. Luckily he'd had the sense then to fight it and to fend her off with an intentionally cruel act. He still regretted laughing at her, but only because he knew it hurt her feelings. Avoiding any physical contact with her was one of the wisest things he could have ever done.

That was just as true today as it was then. One kiss from Felicia would whet an appetite in him that he could never satisfy—especially now that he was a few hours from delivering her to another man's arms. He wanted to curse.

He wanted to throw Felicia in the car caveman-style and keep driving her until she saw that Todd Armstrong was not the man for her. Given enough time and enough tenderness, surely he would persuade her that she could love him.

He chuckled at his own foolishness. Love him? Maybe. But live with him? Who was he kidding? He had nothing to offer a woman like Felicia Grantham except the service she had solicited from him. The only good he was to her was as a means to get to the man she had chosen.

He glanced back over his shoulder to see if her plan had been set in motion. When he saw that it had, he sighed. No going back now, he told himself, and plunged into his part of the strategy.

"No turning back now," Felicia murmured the moment one of the TV reporters spotted her. She knew he'd spotted her because he'd stopped dead in his tracks, an open soda can halfway to his mouth, and stared right at her.

She secured her veil in place with one hand and batted her lashes in her best come-hither fashion. Slowly, as if performing a sensuous exotic dance, she extended her free arm and beckoned the man with the curve of her finger.

"What are you gawking at, Jim?" Felicia heard the heavier of the two young men grumble as he approached his mesmerized companion.

"A mirage," Jim mumbled back.

"A what?" The second man chuckled so hard, his rounded belly jiggled the bright red aluminum can he held in his meaty hand. He bowed his head and, still chuckling, began to pry the tab up to open the can. "You've been on this ridiculous Grantham story so long, you're batty."

"Is that so? Well, if you're so sane, Mike, you look over there in the cactus garden." The lean young man swung his arm out to point at Felicia. "What do *you* see?"

The man called Mike jerked his head up, simultaneously pulling back the can's tab. His gaze fastened on Felicia as though it were metal and she a magnet.

For effect, she rocked her hips and beckoned again.

Mike's can popped open and hissed in warning just seconds before spewing dark, frothy liquid in his face and all over his shirt. In response, Mike spewed a string of foul words.

Felicia bit her lip to keep from laughing. All the while she strained to find Ethan in the parking lot. The second she saw him waving the antenna to the news van's cell phone, she dashed behind the building.

"Should we follow her?" she heard one man ask the other.

"Let's at least see what she's up to" was the reply.

Good, she thought. The gravel in the cactus garden crunched under two pairs of feet just as she rounded the far corner of the building. On that side, she dashed past the rows of vending machines to where they had parked the car.

The space was empty. Her heart stopped. Where was Ethan? She scanned the lot but found no sign of the familiar rental car.

"There she is." The heavyset man jabbed an accusing finger in Felicia's direction.

A faint, rolling sensation seized her. She cast her gaze about frantically for the car. How could her beautiful plan have gone so completely awry? Ethan's name formed on her lips.

No. He was in this as deep as she was. What would he gain from foiling their escape—other than the right to say, "I told you so"?

"Why, that..." She gripped her hands on her hips.

"Hey, hold up, lady," the man she'd heard called Jim called out. "What's going on? Why were you trying to get us to follow you?"

Because I'm a darned fool. She gave into the weighty sinking feeling in her chest. Her shoulders slumped forward. She pressed one toe of her canvas shoe to the pavement, preparing to turn and face the music.

Three sharp notes called her attention to a white van idling nearby. Ethan placed his fingers in the corners of his mouth and repeated the earsplitting whistle.

Felicia ran for the battered vehicle. Her feet never faltered even if her thoughts did trip all over themselves.

"What's with the van?" she asked as she jumped inside and slammed the door.

Ethan gunned the reluctant motor. "It's a safety precaution."

Felicia braced herself straight-armed against the dash to keep from being tossed to one side. "Excuse me for pointing out the obvious, but there isn't anything safe about this tub."

"Quit complaining and check to see what your admirers are up to," he ordered even as he merged the van into the highway traffic.

Felicia peered out the window. Behind them, one of the reporters threw his soda can to the ground in anger. The other stood chest to chest with one of the truckers who had volunteered to detain the news hounds. "It doesn't take much imagination to guess that our reporter friend is not happy about having his van penned in by eighteen-wheelers."

"Just wait 'til he tries to call his station on his cellular phone." Ethan nodded to the shiny silver antenna lying on the floor between their bucket seats.

"Or until he tries to use the pay phones and finds them jammed with a long line of truckers." She sat back in her seat and laughed. "And the worst of it is, I don't think they had any idea it was me, the poor things."

"Don't work up too much sympathy for them. If they had placed you, they wouldn't have spared a shred of emotion over hounding your every step."

"Takes one to know one," she teased.

"Don't lump me in with those bloodsuckers." He kept his eyes forward. "I never advocated tabloid journalism."

"You never advocated it?" She tipped her head to the side and put one finger on her cheek. "Hmm. That's a very precise choice of words, Bradshaw. You sound like a man skirting an issue."

He wrapped his hands around the steering wheel. Only the white of his knuckles hinted at his mood as he studied the road and commanded, "Buckle up."

"Ooh, I must have hit a nerve." She pressed her lips together to contain her smile.

This time he looked at her. His blue eyes shot daggers past the creases caused by his hard squint. Still, his voice sounded more exasperated than angry. "Are you going to buckle up or not?"

She sighed. "After I duck in the back of the van and change back into my real clothes."

She pushed up from the seat. Ethan's hand closed over hers.

"Buckle up," he said softly.

She dropped back into the seat. "You didn't bring my other clothes, did you?"

"I handed them to my contact as we traded vehicles," he admitted. "I forgot to get them back."

She laid her head back, squeezing her eyes shut.

"If it's any consolation, you look really terrific just the way you are."

She forced a groan through her clenched teeth.

"Look, Felicia, I'm sorry. As soon as we get to Vegas, I'll get you something else to wear, I swear."

She contemplated telling him she wasn't mad but she simply couldn't. After all, doing that would mean letting him in on her most intimate secret.

Deep inside, she was thrilled that he had misplaced her clothes. Because it gave her the one thing she truly longed for: more time with him.

"You know, of course," she said with just the right hint of disdain, "this throws everything off schedule."

"Off schedule? I didn't know we had a schedule."

"No schedule?" She turned to face him. "Aren't we supposed to be in Vegas in a couple hours?"

Ethan frowned and shrugged. "Yes."

"And wasn't the whole point of going to Vegas to get me to Todd, complete with exclusive pictures?"

Ethan nodded.

"Well, if you think I'm going to allow myself to be photographed at my big reunion in this thing—" she pinched at the sheer fabric covering her thigh "—then you've got another think coming."

A slow grin worked its way across Ethan's face. "So, what's your suggestion for handling this fashion disaster?"

"My suggestion?" She drew herself up, trying to project a far more serious attitude than she felt. "I suggest, Bradshaw, that when we get to Vegas, we find a suitable hotel where I can take a shower and get presentable.

Meanwhile, you go out and get me something proper to wear."

"Then I deliver you to your intended?"

"Then," she said, angling her chin up and hoping her delight would not shine through her words, "then, we get a decent meal and a good night's sleep."

He twisted his head almost violently to gape at her.

"Don't act so surprised," she ordered impatiently. "Look at these huge circles under my eyes."

She stuck her fingers beneath her eyes and tugged downward to emphasize her haggard appearance. "Do you think for one instant that I would let you capture me on film, looking like this, for the whole world to see?"

His smile quirked to one side.

Something very primal deep inside her leapt at the sight. In that place, she suspected he was on to her ruse, even as he shook his head and grunted.

"You're right, Miss High Horse," he said quietly as he turned his attention back to the road. "You're one hell of a sight and I'd be a cad to put you on display for the whole world to ogle."

"Thank you," she whispered. "I think."

"Do you think one night will be long enough for you to regain your *natural* beauty, or will it take two?"

Two nights in a Las Vegas hotel with Ethan Bradshaw. The very thought made her stomach somersault and her lower regions quiver. She folded her arms over the goose-fleshed skin of her bare midriff. One night was too many, she knew, but if she opened her mouth, she did not trust herself to tell him so.

"Not sure?" He raked one hand back over his stark black hair. "Okay. How about this?"

She held her breath.

"Let's count on one more night together and then..."

She bit her lip, her gaze riveted on him.

His wolfish grin subsided but his voice maintained the primitive growl as he finished, "Then we'll just see what happens."

Chapter Ten

"Now lie back on the bed. Relax. No peeking." Ethan helped Felicia onto the queen-size water bed in the center of the cheap motel they'd selected as their hideaway. The water sloshed and the mattress rolled beneath her weight.

"This is silly, Ethan. Why can't I open my eyes?" she protested.

"One last time, it's for effect. Every newspaper, magazine and tabloid currently following your story is spread in front of you on that bed. I want to capture your honest reaction to them on film."

"Fine." She thrust her hands out to locate the papers without seeing them. Above their crinkling, as she situated herself on the bed, she said, "Now, tell me again why I have to give that reaction while dressed in this harem outfit."

He crouched low and aimed the camera. "Because it's a great photo. You, the getup, the trashy media hype, the one step up from sleazy hotel..."

"One step *up* from sleazy?" She fluffed her still-damp hair. "I checked the bathroom over three times for peepholes before I stepped inside the shower."

Ethan chuckled. "So it's not your usual fare. We're using it as a base of operations, not setting up housekeeping."

"Listen, Bradshaw, this place could use a little housekeeping." She tucked her hair behind her ear, then propped herself up straight-armed on her side. "Can I open my eyes now?"

"Just a minute." He didn't need the time to prepare the shot, he just wanted to savor the sight of her a moment longer.

He lowered the camera in his hands. Without her no-nonsense gaze on him, he could study every nuance of her features. He relished the opportunity to memorize the scent of her hair, the rhythm of her breathing, the beckoning glow of her skin, the things lost in the one-dimensional world of a photograph. The things that would be forever lost to him when she married another man. A cold lump settled in his gut at the thought.

"Ethan, it doesn't take this long to *paint* a picture," she whined with a measure of good humor.

"Okay, okay." He raised the camera again and focused on her. "Open your eyes."

"Oh, my gosh!"

Ethan clicked off picture after picture. Felicia gaping at the materials spread before her. Laughing at some of the wild accounts of her disappearance. Pretending to tear up one of the more critical stories about her relationship with her fiancé. And finally, holding up the headline Bob Harding had promised to print.

"The Fugitive Bride," she said, turning the paper to read it after the picture was shot. "I like it. It makes me sound..."

"Flighty?" Ethan set the camera on the nightstand and stood over her.

She scowled at him. "No."

He rubbed his now-clean-shaven jaw. "Driven?"

"No." She tossed the folded paper onto the bed. Her movement sent a ripple across the shoddy water bed. The other papers fanned over the mattress crackled. "Being called the fugitive bride makes me feel . . . free."

"Free?" He certainly hadn't expected that response. He sank to the edge of the bed, sitting on the padded side rail to avoid creating a tidal wave. "Even after all this time together, you still surprise me, princess."

She dipped her chin and cast her gaze up at him through her lowered lashes. "Do I?"

He wobbled on the vinyl sidebar but caught himself before he fell onto the bed. Clearing his throat, he made himself study her forehead to keep from giving in to any stray sexual thoughts this place and her overt flirting might provoke. "Oh, yes, you're full of surprises, Miss High Horse."

She bristled at the name, just as he intended.

"This crazy misadventure—the camping, the disguises, the dodges, the eating in greasy spoons and then not eating at all—you say that makes you feel free?" He looked down his nose at her. "Darlin', you have all the freedom money can buy—you always have."

"On the contrary." She drew her shoulders up.

Despite the fact that the action made the bed jiggle and her breasts bounce, Ethan focused on her haughty demeanor. Silently, he rooted for a resurgence of the old Felicia.

"I don't expect you to understand this," she said in a newly earnest voice, "but money hasn't bought me freedom. It's only afforded my father better cages."

"I know a lot of people who would trade places with you," he said with a sneer, still trying to pick a fight.

"And I know a lot of people I'd gladly trade places with." She bowed her head and fidgeted with the golden coins dangling from her belt. "You, for instance."

Ethan's forced arrogance drained away. A sucker punch to the kidneys would have been more welcome right now than this humble confession. He narrowed his eyes to block everything but Felicia's downturned face. "Me?" he croaked. "Why would anyone want to trade places with me? All I have is my work record, my memories and a few belongings. I don't even have a real home until I build it."

"But they're all yours."

"What does that mean?"

"It means they belong solely to you—no one gave them to you, no one can take them away. You created them." She sighed as though the world were on her slender shoulders, then lifted her head to look him in the eye. Black curls clung to her neck and seemed to spill over one shoulder like inky rivulets staining her olive-skinned breast. She bit her lip, then let it slide slowly from her white teeth, saying. "I never created a darned thing in my entire life."

"Except havoc," he whispered. He reached out and caught a strand of her hair in his fingers. "And desire."

Following the forward movement and his own instincts, he slid from his seat on the padded bed rail onto the bed. Already, he could smell her fresh skin, her shampooed hair. His senses became both more intense and yet selective. The only distractions breaking through were hers. Papers crunched under his knees as he closed in on her. He didn't care that the newspapers were getting torn and wrinkled. The mattress undulated. He only noticed because it made her body roll toward him. He reached for her.

The dark circles of Felicia's eyes opened as if to take in the whole image of him moving over her. Her lips parted. She arched her back but did not retreat from his advance.

He splayed his fingers, thrusting them through her thick hair to cradle her head in his hands. His gaze penetrated the innocent turmoil in her eyes, at once calming the questions he found there and igniting a guarded flame.

Just before his mouth closed over hers, she said his name. The flick of her tongue as she formed the syllables teased his lips.

This close was not close enough. Kneeling over her, he pulled her up in a tight embrace, skimming one open palm down her silky outfit and warm skin to brace her back. His own tongue touched hers. He probed gently at the plump center of her lower lip and, finding her willing, plunged inside.

Bad idea, a voice in the recesses of his reason shouted.

Nothing too bad could feel this good, he argued. He deepened the kiss, tempting her to burn him with her pent-up fire.

She moaned and wound her arms around his neck, pulling him downward until their bodies met and sank into the swashing mattress.

He pressed his lips to hers, harder than before. He slipped his tongue between her lips again and ground his hips to hers, telling her without words what he wanted. He would make love to her now as he couldn't fifteen years ago when she was still a girl. He would make love to her again and again until his love had obliterated all thought of the man she had come here to marry.

That single thought proved more effective in dousing his passion than an ice-cold waterfall ever could. He'd brought Felicia all this way to marry another man and, through it all, she'd shown no sign of changing that plan. With gargantuan effort, he pushed up from her and stared into her glazed eyes.

"This has gone far enough, princess." He rolled off the bed and stood, his back to her. "You better get dressed."

Stunned and embarrassed by Ethan's rejection, only slightly less brutal than the one fifteen years ago, Felicia leapt up from the bed. She snatched up the plastic shopping bags containing the clothes he'd bought for her earlier in the day and dashed to the bathroom.

The door slammed between them before she allowed herself to think about what had just happened. Tears stung her eyes at how easily she'd been made a fool. Suddenly, the feelings of being sixteen and unsure of her own feminine appeal and tumultuous emotions flooded back. She pressed her back to the cold painted door and bit her lip to hold in a sob.

"Felicia?" Ethan's gentle tapping on the door vibrated down her spine.

"What?" She cursed the telltale emotional warble in her voice.

"I...I didn't mean to hurt your feelings. The old hormones just started kicking up and it took me a while to rein 'em in."

Ethan's stupid cowboy euphemism instantly helped her replace her old insecurities with mild irritation. "If that's supposed to make me feel better, it needs work."

A rumbling laugh answered her. "Well, isn't that typical Miss High Horse? I can't even apologize to suit you."

"Apologize?" She flung open the door. "Ethan Bradshaw, if that was an apology, then please consider this my way of accepting it."

She raised her hand to slap the smug grin right off his cocky face.

"Whoa." He caught her by the wrist. "Is that any way to treat your rescuer, princess?"

"Rescuer? More like my tormentor. Why, you're the most..."

The twinkle in his eye made her stop. He'd baited her and she'd fallen for it. Now she didn't know whether to kick him in the shins as she had as a child or to join him in a mutual chuckle over it. She opted for the latter and let a soft giggle bubble up from the depths of her stomach.

"This is the way it should be between us, princess, and you know it." He dropped her arm. "The only friction we should be generating should be in a heated argument."

She sighed and shook her head. "Do you really believe that, Ethan? Really?"

"Really," he whispered.

She wasn't convinced. Folding her arms across her chest, she leaned back against the doorframe. "Why?"

He dipped his head and cleared his throat. Without looking at her, he answered, "Well, for starters, you're engaged to another man."

"But what if I wasn't?"

"But you are," he bellowed, jerking his head up to glare into her eyes.

She blinked at his overly strong reaction to her simple question. Her knees went weak at the prospect of what this could mean. "But if I wasn't engaged, what would have happened on the bed just now?"

Fire flashed in his blue eyes. He fell forward in a sudden, forceful lunge over her until, at the last possible second, he caught himself. The sound of his hands hitting the wooden doorframe made her jump. He held himself there, his body so close, she could feel its heat on her chest and thighs. It made a strange contrast to the chill from the bathroom at her back.

He leaned his face closer still. The aroma of coffee lingered on the warm breath bathing her lips. He tucked his chin down and a lock of his freshly washed hair brushed her forehead.

"If you weren't engaged," he said, as though it took great effort to speak, "I would have peeled that sexy harem costume off your gorgeous body and explored you so thoroughly, I'd know every freckle and curve blindfolded."

She swallowed—hard.

"Then," he went on in a husky growl, "I would have made love to you."

He inched his face so close that when he blinked, she couldn't help mimicking it.

"We would have made love together," she whispered.

"That's right. We would have made wild, passionate love together—over and over again until we were either dead or loco." He inhaled, taking the breath right out of Felicia's mouth.

When he released it, it was as if a spell had been broken. He pushed away from the doorframe and straightened. "I can't experience that with you today and then watch you marry another man tomorrow. I'm not made like that, Felicia."

"I'm not made like that either, Ethan." Her voice trembled. "And I think you know it."

"What are you saying, Felicia?"

"That I couldn't make love with you and then marry anyone else on earth—ever."

"Ever?" He cocked his head.

"Ever."

"Then it's a good thing we didn't make love, isn't it?"

"Is it?" Her heart pounded in her ears. She clutched at his tensed arms. "Is it a good thing, Ethan?"

His face looked pale and taut. "You're asking the wrong person. Have you completely forgotten the man you love?"

"No, I haven't forgotten him." She stepped up to him and laid her cheek on his chest. "I'm asking him."

"You're asking..." He grabbed her by the shoulders and held her away, his gaze searching her eyes. "Me? You love me?"

She could only nod.

"But how? When?"

"Ever since I can remember, practically." She laughed. She'd never imagined how wonderful it would feel to say it finally. "Being with you these past few days has only confirmed it for me."

"How can that be?" He gripped her shoulders in one firm but gentle shake, as though he were trying to wake her. "Two days ago you were in love with Armstrong."

"I was never in love with Todd." She crossed one arm over her body to place her hand atop his.

"But you said..."

"No, you assumed." She patted his hand and raised her eyebrows at him. "And shame on you for doing it, Mr. Pulitzer Prize winning journalist."

"Then what was all this farce about having to get to Vegas to marry him?"

"That was no farce." But perhaps the connection she'd felt with Ethan was. Even though he'd said he couldn't make love with her then let her marry Todd, he wasn't acting very pleased about her profession of love. Had she made yet another emotional error where this man was concerned? Would her heart take a beating because of it? Hot tears burned above her lower lashes. She blinked them back and tried to concentrate on answering Ethan's question. "When we set out on this adventure, I planned to marry Todd. But it was to be a business arrangement, not a love match."

"Business?" One dark brow arched high. "I don't get it."

"Todd needed money, I needed a husband." She shrugged.

"Felicia, you're not...?" His hand went to her flat stomach.

"Have I acted like a pregnant woman?" She batted his hand away. "When I say I needed a husband, I meant as a legal buffer against my father's interference in my life."

"I still don't get it."

"You wouldn't." She crossed her arms over her chest. "You've always made your own way in life—always able to do as you pleased, to make your own decisions and mistakes."

"And you haven't?"

"Haven't you listened to a thing I've said these past few days? My father, bless his well-intentioned, overprotective heart, has governed my every move. He chose my schools, my friends, my dates—"

"Until Todd," Ethan interjected wryly.

"Oh, I managed to evade Father's grasp a few times," she said with a smile. Then her mood shifted back to the serious topic. "But it never lasted long. Finally I realized that I needed a third party to intervene with Father."

"You honestly think your father would respect Todd enough to entrust him with watching over you?" Ethan ran his finger along her cheek.

"I don't need watching over." She feigned nipping his fingertip.

"My mistake," Ethan muttered, withdrawing his hand. "So, just how was Todd the Clod going to help you handle your father?"

She tried not to smile at Ethan's jealousy over her relationship with the bodybuilder. Perhaps there was hope yet. "This may sound complicated, but what I needed from Todd was someone who could legally block my father's meddling."

"Can you give me an example?"

"I can give you a perfect example." She squared her shoulders and angled her chin up at him. "If Todd and I had been married when Father carted me away from that wedding chapel, then Todd could have filed kidnapping charges."

"Why couldn't you do that yourself?"

"Because I never would—and Father knows that. While Todd, on the other hand..."

"Is just sleazy enough to go for it."

She touched the tip of her nose to show that he'd guessed correctly. "He was perfect for keeping my father in check. Brilliant, yes?"

Ethan shook his head. "Sounds like a good way to get yourself disinherited to me."

"Fine by me." She shrugged again.

"Fine?" His brow pleated down over his startled gaze. "Then how would you take care of yourself? What would you do for money?"

"What everybody does," she snapped. "I'd get a job. I'm not afraid of hard work, Ethan. I thought you'd realized that these past few days."

"My head is reeling from all the things I've learned in the past few minutes. Don't start holding me accountable for the last few days' information until I adjust to this."

She hung her head. "I hoped you'd do more than simply adjust."

"Huh?"

She heaved a ragged sigh. "Ethan, I told you I love you, and you didn't even respond except to grill me about my relationship with Todd."

"Let me explain something, princess." He stepped close and lifted her chin with one finger.

Here it comes. I couldn't take a hint. No, I had to force him to tell me to my face that he has no interest in me other than getting to my father. She grit her teeth to wall in any impulsive remarks she might later regret and raised her gaze to his.

His lips twitched in a half smile. His blue eyes warmed. He started to say something.

Her heartbeat quickened. Could it be?

He shut his mouth. A darkness passed over his features. He shook his head. "You've led a sheltered life—you've admitted as much to me time and again."

"Yes," she managed to say, her lower lip trembling.

"Well, I've been around enough to know that you can't make all your big decisions in life based just on how you feel about something—or someone."

She pulled her chin from his hand. "I don't understand what you're trying to tell me."

"I'm telling you that no matter how you feel right now, no matter how much you think you love me..."

"I do love you," she whispered. He didn't have to profess love he didn't feel, but she'd be damned if she'd let him dismiss her own emotions.

His face went rigid, but his gaze remained soft. "Love doesn't ensure happiness, Felicia."

"Ever try being really happy without it?"

He tipped his head in concession to her point. "Now let me ask you, have you ever tried being happy with nothing else?"

She held her hands up and shook her head slowly.

"That's what being in love with me would mean, Felicia. I'm at the point in my life when all I want is to build a home, settle down, maybe marry and have a family. I hope to get together enough land for a small ranch again. That's my future, and it's pretty dull compared to the life you're destined to lead."

"It sounds like heaven." She laid her hand on his chest. His heart pounded hard against her palm.

"Right now it sounds like heaven, but six months from now..."

Tears spilled over onto her cheeks. "It will still be heaven."

"Felicia, no..."

"Oh, Ethan, haven't you gotten to know me better than that by now? You act like I'm still an overindulged child."

He frowned but remained silent.

She clenched her hand, crumpling the crisp cotton of his new shirt. Despite the heavy sinking in her stomach, she forged on with her argument. "I'm not a kid anymore. I know my own mind and what I want for my life."

He shook his head and started to speak, but she wasn't finished.

"Ethan, I've done the nightlife thing, the society thing, the charity thing, the traveling all over the world pretending I have an exciting and glamorous life thing. *That's* what bores me."

He narrowed his eyes at her and curved his large hand around her shuddering shoulders.

In the safety of even this gentle embrace, she sighed. "Starting a new life, on my own terms with the man I love—building my *own* home..." She glanced down, feeling embarrassed yet secretly cozy in confession, "Having children, our children, would be real happiness for me."

"If only I could believe you." The words rushed out with a long exhale.

Felicia jerked her head up. Her hand clutched at Ethan's shirt. "You can believe me, Ethan. You can."

"No, I can't," he said in a soft, sad voice. "I wish I could. But until I can..."

She swallowed, pushing down a hard knot that had welled up inside her throat. "Until? Does that mean there's hope?"

He smiled. "There's always hope."

She forced her reluctant lips into an answering smile. "Then I'll keep hoping."

Chapter Eleven

"Are you crazy or am I, princess?" Ethan glanced over at Felicia's sleeping form on the bed. He shifted his weight and the wobbling chair beneath him groaned.

He rubbed his palm up the back of his neck, then scored his fingers through his hair. Could he really be considering her claim that she could not only love him but also make a home with him?

Try as he might to put the whole ludicrous idea out of his head as the day progressed, it kept popping back in at the most inopportune times. When they shared a delivered pizza, her enthusiasm for the ordinary fare made him wonder if she could adapt to his life-style. Later, as they watched a daytime talk show, her opinion of the topic had echoed his own. Could they have more in common than he wanted to believe? Finally, when last night's travel had caught up with her, had she balked at resting in the shabby water bed? No, she'd simply thrown open the sheets to inspect them for cleanliness—just as he would have—and then crawled in and fallen asleep.

Now, as he watched her napping, he couldn't help speculating. Had he been wrong about her? It didn't take a leap of faith to admit she'd been right about one thing—she wasn't a kid anymore. He hadn't bothered to do the math before but given that she was about eight years younger than he, that made her...

"Old enough to know what she wants and to take responsibility for that choice." He leaned forward in his chair.

She mewed in her sleep and snuggled her rose-tinged cheek against the white pillow. The sight grabbed him by the heart and gave a sharp squeeze. If he were honest with himself, she'd had his heart in her pretty little hands the whole time. Only circumstances and his own prejudices against her and her father had prevented him from admitting it.

So much had changed. He no longer hated Gower Grantham. Ethan realized the tycoon had only done business with the older Bradshaw, he hadn't done him in. And, in the long run, it had been good business for both families.

As for Felicia... He gazed at her, struggling to keep his breathing even. Well, his opinion of her seemed to change hourly. But one thing remained constant—he loved the woman, temper fits, wisecracks, impulsiveness and all.

She sighed in her sleep.

He felt a grin tug at his lips and he sighed, too.

"Damn it all, I do love you, Felicia," he whispered. "But what am I supposed to do about it?"

He wasn't going to deliver her to Todd Armstrong tomorrow, that was for certain. That would surely put a crimp in his story, he supposed. Wearily, he reached for the plain beige telephone on the table beside him and dialed.

When Bob Harding came on the line, he decided to be direct, honest and unapologetic for the turn of events. "Bob? The story is dead."

"Dead? What do you mean dead?"

"Shh." Ethan put his finger to his own lips as though Bob's screeching might awaken Felicia. "I mean, belly-up, bought the farm, rest in peace, Elvis has left the planet. It's done for."

"Why? How?"

"Why? Because life is wonderfully unpredictable, my friend. How?" He cleared his throat. "How is a funny story."

"Good, I could use a laugh right now."

"Well, you see, Ms. Grantham isn't going to marry Todd Armstrong now."

"When is she going to marry him?"

"Never."

"Oh, for..." Bob garbled a curse. "This is another one of her bullheaded stunts, isn't it? Her dad announces he'll give his blessing to the union if she'll just come out of hiding, and suddenly she chucks her wedding plans."

"Her father did what? When?"

"Held a press conference about an hour ago. Had Armstrong right beside him. Grantham said if she'd just call and let them come get her, he'd throw her a big society wedding with all the trimmings."

"Well, I'll be." Ethan scratched his head in amazement at the new development.

"You didn't know?"

"I didn't know and neither did Felicia. I swear to you, her father's peace offering didn't have a thing to do with her change of heart."

"Then why in heaven's name isn't she marrying Armstrong?"

"Because she's marrying me," Ethan answered through a grin so big, it almost hurt his cheeks.

"What?"

Ethan had to hold the phone away from his ear. "Calm down, Bob."

"Calm? How can you ask me to be calm when you've just dropped the scoop of the week in my lap?"

"I did no such thing, Harding. This story is personal, not for public consumption."

Felicia stirred behind him. The water bed swished beneath her rolling weight. Ethan held his breath and waited for her to settle. When he was sure she wasn't rousing, he continued.

"As I said, Bob, this is my story now. Not yours."

"I provided you with transportation and gave you money to carry off this great escapade. At least I deserve some kind of exclusive out of it. I acted in good faith, Ethan. That used to count for something with you."

He had a point. His personal code of ethics required he honor his promise to deliver a story. "Okay, Bob. How about this? I'll come over right now and pound out my side of the story for you—with one stipulation."

"And that is?"

"You don't print a word or run a single photo until I give the go-ahead."

"I don't know, Bradshaw...."

"I just want time to give Felicia a proper proposal, that's all."

"Can we have a photographer handy? You on one knee before the fugitive bride would make great copy."

"You have ink in your veins, don't you, Bob?"

The man responded with a hard chuckle. "Okay, we sit on the story until you approve it and no proposal photos, but grant me this. . . ."

"I'm afraid to ask."

"Exclusive rights to your wedding pictures."

"Done."

"Done," Bob echoed.

"Felicia's sleeping now." Ethan glanced over to make sure that was still true. Her steady breathing and serene expression reassured him. "I think I can come on in now, write the story and be back before she wakes up."

"Okay, but be careful driving over. I'm telling you, this city is crawling with press. I wouldn't be surprised if your motel is staked out or the staff has been bribed to watch for you."

"Thanks for the warning but I think it's okay. We've been here all day without any trouble."

"Just don't take anything for granted, Bradshaw. I will not take kindly to being scooped on this story."

"No problem, Bob. I've got Felicia hidden well enough to foil the tabloid vultures."

Ethan hung up, then hurried out, hoping he was right about Felicia being safe from any disreputable news hounds.

"Ms. Grantham?"

Felicia sat bolt upright, startled from a deep sleep by the sound of someone knocking on a door. She blinked to acclimate herself to the strange surroundings and the even stranger sensation of the mattress beneath her rolling and sloshing. Where was she?

"Ms. Grantham? Please open the door. Ethan Bradshaw sent me here to get you."

"Ethan," she murmured, thrashing her arms and legs to free herself from the bedcovers and the motion of the mattress. She climbed out of the bed and glanced around the room. The thick, lined curtains blotted out all but a faint outline of the late-afternoon sun. On the nightstand, a digital clock confirmed that it was shortly after five.

"Ethan?" she called, squinting in the dim light toward the open bathroom door. "Are you here?"

"Ms. Grantham?" a feminine voice on the other side of the motel room door asked again. "Ms. Grantham, I work with Mr. Bradshaw. He sent me here for you."

"Oh." She pressed her hands over her temples and rubbed briskly to dispel the fog in her head.

"Let me in and I'll explain everything," the voice coaxed.

"Um, okay. I guess that'll be all right." Out of habit, she checked herself over in the mirror. "Good thing Ethan isn't here to see me after all."

She tried to smooth down her wild mane of hair. Of course, Ethan had seen her looking worse during their time together, but now that she had professed her love for him, her appearance suddenly mattered more. A sweet warmth washed from her chest downward at just the hope that her confession to Ethan might alter their relationship. She crossed her arms over the red cotton sweater Ethan had selected for her and hugged herself.

"Ms. Grantham?"

She jumped. "Oh, I'm sorry, I got sidetracked."

As a precaution, she slid the heavy brass chain on the door guard into place. It clattered as she opened the door just a crack to see her visitor.

A woman with bright blond hair stepped forward, nudging the dented metal door open until the chain stretched to its limit, clacking as it locked the door guard into place.

"I'm sorry," Felicia said, peering under the taut chain. "I didn't catch your name."

"Joan Daly, Ms. Grantham. Ethan Bradshaw sent me here to speak with you."

Felicia cocked her head and studied the flashy blonde. "Something about this doesn't ring true. I'm not speaking to anyone until Ethan gets back."

She started to shut the door, but the woman bodily blocked the move. "I'm afraid you'll have a long wait, then, Ms. Grantham."

Felicia froze. "What does that mean?"

"Mr. Bradshaw isn't coming back. He's left the story and I've inherited the assignment."

"That's a lie," Felicia cried, yanking the door open. The latch caught again and jarred her shoulder all the way up to her jaw. "That's a lie," she said again, quietly. "Ethan wouldn't just go off and leave me."

The woman's expression went soft in contrast to her harsh makeup. "He didn't go off and leave you, he sent me to take care of everything."

"I...I don't believe you." At least she didn't want to believe the woman.

"I know it's a bit unusual. But it's true. How else would I have known where to find you if Ethan Bradshaw hadn't told me?"

"Did he give you a message to give me? Something that would let me know you're legit?"

Joan Daly's smile appeared frighteningly sunny. "No, he just said that shortly after you two finished your double pepperoni pizza..."

"You know we had a double pepperoni pizza," Felicia muttered, her hand closing tightly over the icy doorknob.

"Of course I do," Joan cooed. "I told you, Ethan sent me."

"B-but why?"

"Well, once your father and your fiancé made their public announcement, he said his angle on the story was shot. I'm here to find out when and where the reunion will take place."

"Wait." She held her hand up. "What public announcement? What reunion? What are you talking about?"

"The announcement about your father consenting to your marriage. I have the statement right here." She waved a computer printout sheet in the air. "Why don't you let me in and I'll read it to you?"

If her brain could have conceived anything to say, she could never have forced the words past the huge lump in her throat. Stiffly, she edged the door closed and slid the chain from its brass notch. That done, she opened the door for the cheerful newswoman.

"Thanks for letting me in Ms. Grantham—may I call you Felicia?"

Felicia nodded numbly. "Now, what was that statement from my father you said you had, Ms. Daly?"

Joan pushed the door shut behind her. "Call me Joan."

"Okay, Joan." She smiled weakly in the woman's direction, her hands wadding the hem of her new sweater.

"The announcement was made at a joint press conference earlier this afternoon." As she spoke, Joan swept through the room. When she seemed satisfied with her perusal, she turned on her pump heel and nailed Felicia with a hard glare. "Bradshaw didn't tell you anything about it?"

"Um, no." The stretchy cotton fabric of her hem conformed to her curled fingers as she twisted it. "I was worn-out from the traveling and I fell asleep. He probably didn't want to wake me."

"Well, he's thoughtful that way, isn't he?" Joan never raised her eyes from the pad where she was rapidly scribbling notes.

A shudder ran down Felicia's spine. She released the sweater in her fist and pulled her shoulders back. "You say it like you think Ethan's anything but thoughtful."

The woman shrugged and made her eyes wide in a look of peculiar sympathy. "How thoughtful can he be, Felicia? He didn't even bother to tell you this momentous personal news. He just saw his part was done and took off—like he was the one running away from something."

To say the accusation struck a nerve would be a vast understatement. It pierced her heart—but then the truth had a way of doing that, didn't it?

Ethan had run out on her. She'd confessed her love for him and, like all those years ago, he'd rejected her with anguishing finality.

Felicia struggled to make sense of it all. "But why would he just give you the story when he had all those pictures?"

"Pictures?" Joan's head snapped up. "Did he have a lot of pictures? What were they of?"

"Me, mostly." Felicia seized the glimmer of hope this woman's reaction generated. Maybe this was all a big mistake or a competitor trying to weasel in on Ethan's exclusive. "But shouldn't you know about the pictures if you're picking up the story from where he left off?"

"Oh, *those* pictures." Joan waved her hand in a dismissive gesture. "I can understand your confusion, but the reason I don't have any specifics on those photos is because Bradshaw refused to hand them over to our chief."

"He did?" The glimmer of hope became a beacon.

"Sure. Are you kidding?" The woman shrugged and leaned in as if confiding in Felicia. "Do you know what those picture are worth on the open market? Bradshaw expects to really clean up, it'll more than make up for his trouble getting you this far."

"And hold me and my father up to public ridicule." Her hope was all but extinguished.

"Yes, it looks like Bradshaw milked the situation for all it was worth and then got out. He took you for a ride in more than one way."

Felicia flinched and bit her lip to keep from launching a denial that even she would find implausible.

"That's right, isn't it, Felicia? Bradshaw used you, then ran. I just wonder *why* he ran." Joan tapped her pen to her cheek, but her gaze remained riveted to Felicia's face. "Do you have any insights into that?"

Felicia's lower lip trembled under her teeth. Fat tears sparkled in her line of vision. Not even a sob could escape her chest—the ache was so great there.

"What happened, Felicia? Did you and Bradshaw fight about something?"

The eagerness in the newswoman's tone served as a warning to Felicia. With great effort, she raised her chin and called upon the polished persona that life and her father had demanded of her. "If you would be so kind, Ms. Daly, as to read my father's statement?"

The woman's eyes narrowed. Her jaw jutted forward. Clearly, she did not respond well to having her questions ignored or to being dictated to.

Felicia didn't care. She had just learned that the man she loved had deserted her without even a goodbye. And he'd left her in a crummy motel in a strange town with no money. After all her proclamations of independence and being in control to Ethan, the time had truly come for her to prove what she was made of.

She pulled her shoulders up. She'd show him. She'd show everyone. She snatched the paper from Joan Daly's hand. "Here, let me read it myself, then."

She scanned the two-paragraph statement twice, then let the thin page somersault to the grungy shag carpet at her feet.

"Your father has pleaded with you to contact him, Felicia. He's agreed to throw you a fantasy wedding to the man of your dreams, Todd Armstrong. Do you have a response?" Joan stepped forward, her pen poised.

"It seems I don't have any options," she said in what felt like regal resignation. "Now, if you'll excuse me, I have to call my father."

Chapter Twelve

"Damn Felicia Grantham, her arrogant father *and* her musclehead of a future husband." Ethan stomped inside his rattletrap trailer and slammed the door. He'd been back from Las Vegas a week but Felicia's betrayal still stung like a fresh wound. What a fool he'd been to think that Miss High Horse would come down from her perch to live the simple life with him.

"One offer of something better and wham—" He brought his fist down on the faded red countertop. "She was out the door so fast, she couldn't even stop to say goodbye."

The sinking sensation of walking into the empty motel room haunted him. More disturbing still, was the memory of turning on the TV later to see Felicia standing between her father and her fiancé, apologizing to total strangers for any inconvenience she might have caused.

"But did she apologize to me?" he muttered. No. Apparently she felt his inconvenience was as easily dismissed as her so-called feelings for him.

Not to mention, he thought, the "inconvenience" of having every last guest invited to Felicia's wedding this afternoon drive right past his home. He wiped a rivulet of sweat from his neck. He'd thought working on the cabin would provide the needed release for his pent-up hostility.

Then the stream of cars had begun. First the florist and catering vans, then photographers. Those he could stand, but when the media started to descend, he had to beat a nasty retreat inside. His pride would not allow suffering through rogue reporters intruding on him to ask for his take on the society wedding.

At least he'd been able to kill his own ridiculous story about his adventure with Felicia and their subsequent romance. Thoughts of the article drew his attention to a big manila envelope resting on the tiny table of his cramped trailer.

In one step he stood over the offending packet—the photographic account of the trip he once thought had changed his life. He picked up the envelope and stared at it. His pulse pounded in his ears with every hammer of his aching heart. How could he have been so wrong about her? How could he have loved such a mercenary, self-centered...

He gripped the envelope with both hands, planning to rip it in half and then in quarters, as if that could destroy all evidence of his association with Felicia Grantham.

Outside, the rumble of several passing cars made him pause. Still clutching the pictures, he leaned over and pushed aside the curtains to peer at the arriving guests.

The wedding would be starting soon. He narrowed his eyes at the cars winding down the road toward the Grantham ranch. His chest constricted and he imagined it compressing his pain into a detached sense of purpose. He didn't need Felicia Grantham. He was well rid of her. And to prove it, he'd go over and kiss the greedy little bride goodbye. He clenched his fist, and the envelope in his hand crinkled.

"And I know just what to give the happy couple for a wedding present."

Any minute now, he's going to burst in here and call a halt to this whole charade. Felicia paced the length of her bedroom and back again. The stiff fabric of her bell-shaped slip whisked over the plush carpet, agitating her nerves further. She focused her gaze on the intricately beaded lace wedding dress spread over her queen-size bed. Tugging up the top of her strapless bra, she spun to face the door.

Where was her father, and why hadn't he stormed in to insist this farce of a marriage be called off? How could he have let it go on this far? If he didn't show up soon, she was going to have to pull another flaky stunt to keep the pointless ceremony from proceeding.

She didn't want to marry Todd Armstrong. She would not. She had no intention of marrying anyone—ever. An image of Ethan's flashing blue eyes and heart-stopping smile formed in her mind.

She pressed her eyes shut so tightly that the tears had to roll along her mascaraed lashes to escape. But that did not squeeze the bittersweet intruder from her thoughts.

"Leave me alone." The cry rose from her anguished heart. She placed her fists at her temples. "Get out of my head, Ethan Bradshaw, and go straight to—"

"Here comes the bride..."

Felicia gasped at the off-key melody wafting from the other side of her bedroom door. How dare Ethan Bradshaw show his face in her home today!

"Back from her wild ride..."

She stormed to the door and flung it open.

"I'm sorry, Ms. Grantham," one of the hired ushers said over Ethan's shoulder. "But he pushed past and insisted on seeing you."

"But even I didn't imagine how much of you I'd be seeing." Ethan gave her undressed state a casual perusal, his nonchalance echoed in his stance, as he leaned against the doorframe.

Felicia's emotions soared and crashed all in the same instant. Having Ethan so near thrilled her beyond reason, yet tore at her heart like some cruel beast. Avoiding Ethan's eyes, she glanced at the usher, dismissed him with a nod and spoke what she hoped was the truth. "It's okay. I can handle this."

The usher returned her nod and left.

Drawing herself up, she swallowed the turmoil rising in her chest and demanded, "What do you want, Bradshaw?"

"Hello, Felicia. Looks like you're wearing considerably more for your second attempt at marrying Armstrong than you did the first time."

She crossed her arms over her chest, well aware that the long, full half-slip and satin-and-lace bra did in fact cover more skin than her harem outfit had. She tipped her chin up and rasped, "What are you doing here?"

"My, my. I believe this impending marriage has improved your disposition, Felicia. After you become Mrs. Todd Armstrong, you should be downright surly."

"If you've come here to provide the entertainment, Bradshaw, you should know we don't need a clown."

"I know—you already have Todd the Clod." He chuckled softly.

She wanted to slap him. Her hand trembled open at her side. From somewhere in her battered being, she found restraint. "Maybe you should just leave."

"Without kissing the bride?" He feigned surprise, then let his smile shift into something of a leer. "I wouldn't dream of it."

"That's enough." She managed to sound like she meant it, even while battling the whirling sensations of pain, euphoria and anger. "Please leave."

"Nope." He pushed by her.

As he passed, she caught the familiar scent of his aftershave. With his back to her, she could see the dampness on the waves of hair brushing his collar. He must have just showered and slipped into that well-fitting denim shirt and nearly new black jeans before coming over. What had made him take such an impulsive action, she wondered. Her mind reeled with speculation.

"I'm not leaving until I do what I came here to do," he said, as if answering her unspoken question.

"What?" she rasped.

"Deliver my wedding present to the happy bride." He held a big brown envelope up.

She laced her arms under her breasts as if to protect herself from what was to come. "It looks too flat to be a bomb. What is it?"

"Not a bomb, my dear—a bombshell." He tossed the envelope on top of her waiting wedding gown. "These are the pictures from our little misadventure."

Her breath caught high in her chest. "That's it? You horned in on my wedding day just to hand me some photos that I'll be able to see in next week's tabloid newspapers anyway?"

The sparkle in his eyes took on an icy calm. "You won't see these in next week's tabloid or the week after's."

"Oh? So you sold them to a more reputable magazine?"

He stepped forward, leaning over her just enough to make her tip her head back. "I didn't sell them. Period. But thanks for reminding me that with you everything has to come down to money."

"That's a pretty high-and-mighty attitude for a man whose sole purpose in taking those photos was revenge."

"My motives were less than pure, but at least I had enough of a conscience to do the right thing." He straightened away.

"If you're accusing me of something, Bradshaw, say it."

"Okay, I believe the word is *treachery.*" He set his jaw and glared at her, daring her to deny it.

"Treachery?" she whispered, shaking her head. "I don't know what you mean."

"Sure, just like you didn't know how pretending you loved me would affect me. Or how I might feel coming back to an empty motel room without even a note of explanation or goodbye. And I suppose you didn't understand how it would add insult to injury when you called in a competing reporter to scoop my exclusive story."

It was all too much to handle at once, so she started with the easiest to refute. "I didn't call in Joan Daly—you did."

"Me? Why would I do a stupid thing like that?"

"Because once my father ended the chase, your interest in the story waned." Felicia struggled to keep from whining out the painful tale. "Joan explained the whole thing. You wanted to get away from me, and fast."

"And you believed her," he muttered almost as if speaking to himself.

"Of course I believed her. She knew where I was hiding, she even told me what was on our pizza. How could she have known that if you didn't tell her?"

Ethan groaned and winced. "The pizza delivery guy. I should have thought he might tip off another reporter."

"You mean Joan lied to get my story?"

Ethan's lip curled up into an ironic smile. "You really are too trusting, kid."

"Not anymore." She angled her face up to give an air of finality to her statement.

"Ah, don't say that." He moved close and started to put his finger under her chin.

She jerked her face away from his touch. "If it's one thing I've learned from you, Ethan, it's not to trust anyone."

"That doesn't bode well for your future husband." Ethan dropped his hand to his side, withdrawing emotionally, as well.

Tell him. Tell the man you're not marrying Todd. Perhaps now that he knew she'd been tricked into leaving him, she reasoned, their relationship could still be saved.

"But, then," Ethan went on, "maybe it's better you don't fully trust your groom. This is, after all, still a business arrangement, isn't it?"

"I don't love Todd," she croaked, praying he would seize the chance she was providing for him to turn things around.

"That's just as well, then. Your money and your methods are best suited to that kind of match anyway."

"Get out of my home." *After* he left, she'd break down and sob her eyes out. He could have salvaged everything with three little words. Instead, he'd chosen to torment her. That was answer enough for her hopeful heart. All she wanted now was to get him out of her home and her life forever. She pushed at his solid chest. "Go."

"In that envelope is every picture I took, plus the negatives. They're yours." He gave her a curt nod. "Best wishes on a long and happy union."

He spun on his heel and stormed out the door.

Felicia sank to the bed. Her lace dress rustled under her weight. She didn't care that the elegant gown was getting wrinkled. She didn't care about anything.

Her lip trembled and she bit it to hold in the wail that was building deep in her chest. She threw out one hand to brace herself upright and encountered the envelope Ethan had left.

Anger overcame her heartbreak just long enough for her to grab up the packet. Fate foiled her intention to tear up the pictures unviewed when the envelope fell open and photographs and negatives spilled all over the carpet.

Falling to her knees, Felicia began to push the black-and-white glossies into a pile. There weren't too many. Twenty, maybe, in all. They'd been too constrained by time and the circumstances for more. Drawn to the photos like some sweet forbidden fruit, she began to lay them in order.

The first pictures of her in her harem costume inside Ethan's trailer were followed by her in the stable, her in the diner, her standing beside a pay phone, sticking her tongue out. Then there were assorted poses in and around the pop-up camper, and finally several of her marveling at the media hype she'd caused.

Twenty-two photos. All that remained of her time with Ethan. The tears that had subsided during her musing over the photos threatened to return. To avoid that, she busied herself with gathering up the four strips of negatives and placing them in order, only glancing at the six negatives on each strip.

Six negatives on four strips? She glanced at them again. After accounting for one blank frame, she located the twenty-third negative.

Ethan had lied. He hadn't given her all the photos.

"Felicia, the guests are—" Her father swung open her bedroom door. "Land's sake, child, why aren't you ready?"

She looked up at her father through a veil of tears and, hugging the telltale strip of negatives, she whispered, "He loves me."

"I doubt that muscle-bound clod is capable of love, darling." Her father's chubby cheeks puffed out. "But Todd Armstrong is the one you want so you shall have him."

"Not Todd. Ethan." She inhaled deeply, and for the first time in a week, it didn't hurt. "Ethan Bradshaw loves me."

"What in heaven's name are you talking about?" He swept away the beads of sweat on his bald head with his starched white kerchief. "Why do you think Bradshaw loves you? I thought he deserted you."

"I thought so, too, but I was wrong. And I was wrong when I thought he didn't love me. He does. Why else would he have kept a picture of me for himself?"

"You're not making a lot of sense, Felicia."

"No one in love makes sense, Daddy." She beamed up at her father from her seat on the floor and giggled.

"Daddy?"

Was she mistaken or was there a mist in her father's eyes?

"You haven't called me Daddy since you were a child." The older man scrunched his bushy eyebrows down over his searching gaze.

"Well, get used to it," she announced capriciously. She leapt up from the floor. "Because when I marry Ethan

Bradshaw, not only will I call you Daddy but there will be a bunch of little Bradshaws running around calling you Granddaddy."

"Granddaddy." He threw out his chest—which was actually more stomach than chest—and patted his fingers over his tuxedo lapels. "I like the sound of... Wait just one moment, young lady. Did you say marry Ethan Bradshaw?"

She snatched up her gown and began to step into the ornate creation. "Yes, I did. I'm going to marry Ethan Bradshaw, Daddy. And you can't stop me."

She twisted her arms over her shoulder to try to reach the zipper hanging open midway down her back. Just as her fingertips brushed the cold metal grip, she felt her father's hand encompass hers. The zipper made a low growl as he pulled it closed.

"Am I a complete fool, Daddy?" she asked as she turned to face him.

"Do you love Ethan Bradshaw?"

"With all my heart."

"No one's a fool who goes after something they want that badly." He kissed her cheek. "I had your horse saddled and it's waiting beside the back door."

Her stomach lurched. "Why?"

He shrugged. "Oh, I don't know. It seemed like a nice day for a ride, I suppose."

She laughed. "You knew all along that I would never marry Todd Armstrong."

"Let's just say, I believed you'd do the right thing." He winked at her.

"That means a lot to me, Daddy." She threw her arms around his neck. "I love you."

He patted her back. "You'd better get going. Now that I've given the bride away, there's a few things I'd like to give the ex-groom."

She kissed his cheek again and hurried to finish dressing.

Ethan peeled his freshly pressed denim shirt off and threw it in the dirt. Physical exertion was the only answer to the raw emotion raging in his veins. He stomped over to the tin work shed beside the foundation of his cabin. Clouds of red dust rose from beneath his boots and fell again to cover his footprints.

He'd work until he was so exhausted, he couldn't think of Felicia taking her wedding vows in the ranch down the road. He raised his head to glare in that direction.

"Damn," he muttered. As if Felicia had not been cruel enough.... Now his foolish heart was playing tricks on him. He squinted out onto the dusky horizon and willed the flash of white to disappear. It didn't.

"It can't be." But further scrutiny told him it was. Someone dressed from head to toe in white was barreling toward him. This time he could make out the form, and even though yards of white fabric hung over the horse's flanks and backside, Ethan could clearly see the black animal's head and its flashing hooves.

He shuffled the few feet to the silver tank where his own horse, Hickory, was drinking. He dipped his fingers into the chilly water and flicked some onto his bare chest.

Hickory snorted and pawed the ground.

"What are you looking at?" He glared at the animal. "Haven't you ever seen a man try to look like he's been working up a sweat? I can't let her ride in here and think I was sitting around mooning or something."

The horse gave one big shake of its head, sending its brown mane flailing every which way.

The warm Texas breeze hit the wet sprinkles on Ethan's chest and made him shiver. At least, he told himself, it was the wind and not his anticipation of Felicia's arrival that caused the reaction.

She thundered onto his property and pulled on the reins to stop her horse. She didn't try to dismount but simply sat there, staring down at him with a peculiar expression on her flushed face.

Rather than risk being made a fool of once again by this fickle female, he crossed his arms and uttered the first wisecrack that came to his mind. "If you've come to borrow a cup of rice for your guests to throw at you and Loverboy, I'm all out."

"Fine." She tossed her raven hair and the end of her lace veil whipped in the wind. "Then maybe I'll borrow some stubborn pride. You seem to have a surplus of that stuff."

"You don't need it." He forced out a hard chuckle. "You have more than enough of that already."

"Me?"

Her horse startled at her high-pitched response. Ethan rushed up and clamped his hand on the bridle just above the bit to keep the skittish animal still.

"How can you say I have too much pride?" she asked when the horse calmed. "I'm here, aren't I?"

"As opposed to being where?" He had to know exactly what she was up to before he dared show his hand—or his feelings.

"As opposed to being at my own wedding." She heaved an angry sigh. The crystal beads on her gown picked up the day's fading light and shimmered. The heavy fabric rustled in the brittle silence.

Ethan's gaze sank deeper and deeper into her fathomless eyes. The wind lifted a lock of his hair and blew it across his forehead. He didn't even flinch.

Finally, Felicia groaned in frustration. "Why did I do this?"

"You tell me."

"I came because I thought..."

"You thought what, Felicia? That I'd come running out and sweep you into my arms? That I'd fall at your feet like a fool?"

"I came because I thought this meant something." She tossed the picture packet down. It spun and flipped once in the air before landing with a thud by Ethan's boots.

He didn't know what to say, so he just looked from the envelope in the dust to her face.

"There's a photo missing." She pointed one trembling finger at the packet. "It's of me by a pay phone, smiling right into the camera."

"I remember it," he said. "But I still don't see the connection. Surely you didn't postpone your wedding just to come get that photo."

"I didn't postpone the wedding and I don't want the photo."

"Then why...?"

"I never intended to marry Todd." She bowed her head. "I was just going through the motions of the wedding, waiting for my father to admit he was wrong and call it all off. If he hadn't, I would have."

"Never intended to marry him? Felicia, have you looked in the mirror lately? For a lady saying she doesn't want to get married, you certainly haven't dressed the part."

She smoothed her hand down her gown, her head still bent. "I want to get married—just not to Todd."

Skyrockets went off in Ethan's head. His heart pounded out a booming cadence. Could she really be saying what he thought she was saying?

"I wore the dress because I wanted to make an entrance when I came over to tell you I still loved you. For some reason, I thought the fact you kept my picture meant that you loved me."

She yanked the leather bridle to try to free it from his hand, pulling hard to turn the horse away. "I guess I was wrong."

Ethan wound the bridle tighter in his fist and stood firm. "You weren't."

Her teary eyes flashed at him. "What?"

"You weren't wrong. I do love you." He stepped beside the quieted horse and lifted his arms to her.

She tensed. "If you love me, then why have you been acting like such a jerk?"

He shrugged. "Just my usual charming self, I guess. But then, you're not exactly short on that brand of charm yourself, Miss High Horse."

"Don't call me that."

"You know, sitting up there on that horse in your lace and finery, with that long, flowing veil clinging to your beautiful hair..."

She cocked her head to show her piqued interest.

"You look every bit the royal pain in the butt you are."

"Ooh, you are charming. It's a wonder no girl has snapped you up yet." Her black eyes glistened.

"I don't want a girl," he said, edging closer. "I thought I made that clear to you fifteen years ago."

"Then, what do you—"

One well-timed tug and Ethan had her sliding from the horse and into his arms. The moment her body met his, he pulled her into a tight embrace, one he hoped to never release.

"I want *you.*" He tilted his head to kiss her.

"You want me?" She held her head straight. "You have an interesting way of showing it."

"Actually, I have a very interesting way of showing it." He placed his hands on either side of her face and adjusted her head in perfect position for his purpose.

Felicia squirmed against Ethan's passion.

He fit his mouth to hers.

Who did he think he was? her mind raged. Kissing her like...

He curved his strong arms around her and enclosed her in a circle of warmth and safety.

Like a man in love, she concluded. She splayed her hands over his bare back, reveling in the contrast of smooth skin and taut muscle.

The wind flattened her floor-length veil to her own back, blowing the sheer fabric around the two of them like a curtain to hide them from the whole world.

She deepened the kiss, digging her fingertips into his shoulders. This was it. This was right.

Ethan tore his lips away from hers. "Felicia, are you sure?"

Every fiber of her being sang with joy. "I'm sure."

She leaned forward to kiss him again, but he evaded her. "Ethan, I said I was sure."

He put his forehead to hers. "And that's why we have to stop."

She searched his face. "What now? I thought we worked through it all. We love each other...."

"And that's why we have to stop kissing and start driving."

"Driving?" The wind pulled at her veil and she raised a hand to hold it in place. "Where are we driving?"

"To Vegas," he said in a deadly serious tone.

"Vegas? What for?"

"Because that's where we can get married without further delay."

"Married?" She thought she felt her heart stop. She definitely felt that she was walking on air. Silently she thanked Ethan for lifting her against his body just high enough to put them nose to nose. She doubted if she could have stood on her wobbling legs much longer. "Oh, Ethan, do you mean it?"

"Even I'm not fool enough to propose marriage to a woman in a wedding dress without meaning it." He lowered her slowly to the ground again. "So, what do you say? Will you marry me?"

"Yes, yes, yes!" She threw her arms around him and sent him staggering back a step before he balanced them both. She kissed his cheek, his temple, his earlobe, only pausing to whisper, "You know, we could get to Vegas a lot faster in my daddy's jet. If you don't mind accepting a favor from a Grantham."

Ethan leaned back to look her in the eyes and grinned. "I plan on accepting a lot of favors from a certain Grantham...."

"A former Grantham," she reminded him. "And the sooner she becomes a former Grantham, the sooner those favors begin."

His grin broadened. "Tell Daddy to gas up the jet, Miss High Horse."

"That's *Mrs.* High Horse to you." She brushed his nose with hers. "And don't you forget it, Ethan Bradshaw. Don't ever forget it."

* * * * *

COMING NEXT MONTH

#1132 SHEIK DADDY—Barbara McMahon

Super Fabulous Fathers

Years ago, Sheik "Ben" Shalik had loved Megan O'Sullivan with his whole heart. Now he was back, ready to sweep her off her feet. But could he forgive Megan for keeping their daughter a secret?

#1133 MAIL ORDER WIFE—Phyllis Halldorson

Valentine Brides

Mail order bride Coralie Dixon expected anything from her husband-to-be, except outright rejection! Handsome bachelor Jim Buckley *said* he wasn't interested, but his actions spoke differently....

#1134 CINDERELLA BRIDE—Christine Scott

Valentine Brides

Tall, dark and stirringly handsome, Ryan Kendrick was a perfect Prince Charming. But his "convenient" wedding proposal was hardly the fairy-tale marriage Cynthia Gilbert had been hoping for!

#1135 THE HUSBAND HUNT—Linda Lewis

Valentine Brides

Sarah Brannan was all set to say "I do." But then Jake Logan asked her to *live* with him—not marry him. So Sarah set out to turn the reluctant Jake into her willing groom.

#1136 MAKE-BELIEVE MOM—Elizabeth Sites

Valentine Brides

Prim and proper Laura Gardiner was shocked by rancher Nick Rafland's scandalous proposal. Nick needed a make-believe mom for his little nieces, not a real wife. But Laura wanted to be a true-blue bride....

#1137 GOING TO THE CHAPEL—Alice Sharpe

Valentine Brides

Elinor Bosley ran a wedding chapel, though she'd vowed never to walk down its aisle. Then she met sexy Tom Rex and his adorable four-year-old son. And Elinor started hearing wedding bells of her own!